JUNGLE TALES

AIRSHIP 27 PRODUCTIONS

Jungle Tales-Volume 2
"Ki-Gor and the Smoking Cavern," "Tembu George and the Slavers," "N'Geeso and the Silver Bird" © 2014 John R. Rose

Published by Airship 27 Productions
www.airship27.com
www.airship27hangar.com

Interior llustrations © 2014 Clayton Hinkle
Cover illustration © 2014 Andy Fish

Managing Editor: Ron Fortier
Associate Editor: Gordon Dymowski
Promotions Manager: Michael Vance
Production and design: Rob Davis

ISBN-13: 978-0692293676
ISBN-10: 0692293671

Printed in the United States of America

10 9 8 7 6 5 4 3 2 1

JUNGLE TALES
Volume Two
(FEATURING KI-GOR, LORD OF THE JUNGLE)

By John R. Rose

KI-GOR AND THE SMOKING CAVERN

Two darkly tanned figures, glistening golden in the sunshine, cavorted in a pool of water. Light laughter and giggling carried on the soft breeze wafting across the idyllic setting. Suddenly the man stopped and raised his hand for silence. He shook his head to clear his face of the wet sun bleached white-blond hair as he listened.

"Someone comes," he said softly.

His auburn haired companion ducked her face into the water and stroked rapidly for the bank. The man was beside her as the two silently rose out of the water and onto the shore. Quickly they palmed the dripping water from their nude bodies and donned dry clothing. The man's attire was nothing more than a leopard skin loin cloth. The woman, in addition to the loin cloth, also slipped on a halter top. Picking up their weapons, they faded into the dark shadows of the surrounding jungle.

"I hear it now, Ki-Gor," the girl whispered. "Just one, I think?"

"Yes, Helene," agreed the tall muscular man. "A friend, I believe, as he is making no attempt to conceal his coming."

Although the pair was sure the visitor was a friend, they remained in the shadows, unseen, until they could identify the approaching fellow for certain.

"Tembu George!" exclaimed Ki-Gor softly.

"Hello, George," called Helene, smiling brightly as she stepped out to meet their old friend.

"It has been many days since we have seen you," added the Jungle Lord. "What brings you to this part of the jungle?"

"It occurred to me," the big native said, a pensive look on his face, "that your beautiful wife might be interested to know that the goat, Shuba, has given birth to twins. She is now giving an abundance of milk. Perhaps Helena has another baby monkey?"

They all laughed as they remembered the time when the girl took in a baby green tinted monkey and kept him alive with milk from the nanny goat.

"Helena does not have any babies that she is raising at the moment," smiled Ki-Gor. "But who knows what tomorrow will bring?" Again, the group chuckled.

"George, you will stay and eat with us, will you not?" the young woman asked. "Ki-Gor brought in some fresh antelope and it should be tender by now."

"I would stay," agreed the giant black man with a nod. "There is more that I would discuss with my friend, Ki-Gor and his mate." The man smiled at the two bronzed white people before him. "But it can wait until we are settled down with food."

They walked a short distance to a large Baobab tree that sported a bamboo tree house of multiple levels. It was over thirty feet from the ground up to the lower branches but there was a strong heavy vine hanging down the trunk. Helene grabbed the jungle rope and began pulling herself upward, her feet walking against the trunk as she went upward. When she was among the branches and moving toward the first floor of the tree house, Ki-Gor nodded toward the vine and Tembu George caught the dangling jungle rope and swarmed up the side of the tree. He was followed by Ki-Gor.

On the lower floor of the tree house, they were met by a young cheetah. He came immediately to Ki-Gor and began rubbing against the man's leg.

"I see you have another cheetah," said Tembu George, who was aware of the white man's penchant for taming and training the jungle cat. "What did you name this one?"

Ki-Gor chuckled lightly. "This one is named Hlee-hlee," he said.

"Isn't that the same name as the one that saved Helene from that giant gorilla fella?"

"Yes," the bronze man nodded. "She thought it would be the nice thing to do. I believe Hlee-hlee likes her as much as he does me. Maybe more."

Tembu George nodded and the two men moved to the west side of the platform where they could watch the sun sink in the west surrounded by a red-orange haze.

Later as they finished eating and dusk was fading into darkness, the big black Masai cleared his throat and looked at his two friends. "As the two of you are aware," he said, "I didn't come all this way just to tell you about your old goat having kids. One of my men came to me a day ago and told me about a white man camped in the bend of the Ieka River. That is about a good day's journey from here, if you were riding Marmo. A white man camped in the jungle is not a thing to worry about," Tembu George continued. "However, this fellow had two children with him. They seemed quite young, maybe ten or twelve years old. Not old enough to be running around in the jungle by themselves and there seemed to be no one else with them. Just the man. My scout said there were a few safari members coming and going but the white man just stayed in his camp on the bend of the river. The scout thought there might be some kind of poaching going on, but he did not see that activity."

Ki-Gor nodded, his brows furrowed slightly. "What is your thought, George?" he asked. "You came all this way to tell me about the man. Is this something Ki-Gor should look into?"

"I do not know," replied the warrior chief. "My scout had the feeling that not all was as it seemed in the camp. He thought perhaps the man was waiting on something. Camped on the bend of a river the way he is, is a good way to get washed away if there is a big rain up in the hills!"

"Should we check this out?" Ki-Gor asked, turning toward his red-headed wife.

"I wouldn't mind finding out what the man is doing there," said Helene, "but I don't want to walk all that distance. Do you think we could find Marmo?"

Ki-Gor shrugged. "I can call him in the morning. If he is in the surrounding area and answers me, we could ride him."

The following morning the three friends breakfasted on fresh fruit and strips of dried venison. Then they went down the vine until they were on the ground below the giant tree.

"I would go with you to see this strange man," said Tembu George, "but I can see that you and Helene would like to make this trip together without company. I do not think there is any large amount of danger and I have things I should do back in the village. Perhaps I will come again in a week's time and see how the journey played out."

Ki-Gor gave a slight smile and nodded. "Soon I will call Marmo, the elephant, and see if he is willing to make this journey. If he is somewhere around here, Helene and I will be on our way shortly."

"And if he is not anywhere close?" asked Tembu George, a grin on his face.

"We will just wait until he is," replied Ki-Gor. "If we are to believe there is nothing serious about this journey, then a day or two should make little or no difference."

The big black man nodded. "My scout seemed to think something was going on that he could not see. Be careful, my friend!"

They waved as Tembu George trotted away to the north. The fellow would hold the mile eating gait for hours and the amount of distance he would cover would be amazing.

"I think," said Ki-Gor softly, "George believes there is more to this than what we can see."

"Yes," agreed Helene. "He just didn't know what to tell you the problem might be. But I am sure he thought there was some reason for the strange behavior of the white man."

Ki-Gor grunted and nodded. "Wait here," he said, "I will go up the tree and call Marmo."

"Yes, I don't want to be too close when you give that whistle!" Helena said. "It is really hard on my eardrums."

The bronzed man leaned his assegai against the trunk of the huge Baobab and quickly went up the hanging vine. Shortly Helene heard the sharp piercing whistle, more of an undulating wail than anything else, that Ki-Gor used to summon Marmo. There was a short interval and then it was repeated. The girl was glad she was not standing next to her mate when he made those shrill sounds. Even some distance away, she felt the chills go down her back.

"Ki-Gor," said Helene, when her mate was back on the ground, "this river that you and George talked about, is it the one that has all those rounded stones along the banks?"

The man nodded and smiled. "Yes, it is," he said. "You were there once."

"I thought so," she said. "If we are riding Marmo, would it be alright if I take a couple of sacks and gather some of the stones for decorations in our house? They could serve two purposes," she continued. "In addition to being pretty, they could be used to throw at anything that happened to get into our home! I am thinking of any of the cat creatures that live in the jungle. They could come calling at any time!"

"They would probably be not too eager to enter our tree house," said Ki-Gor, "because of Hlee-hlee. And if he weren't there, the scent of his presence would be enough. But you may gather the stones, if you like. Marmo will not mind carrying them on our return."

"Do you think Marmo will come?"

"It depends on how far away he was," the bronzed man replied. "If he were close, he would be here by about now. If he were some distance away, it will take a little longer."

An hour later, there was still no Marmo and the jungle pair had decided they would wait until the following day to begin their journey.

The red dusk of evening was fading and the sun was already below the western horizon when Ki-Gor saw the dark gray shape in the tropical forest not more than two hundred yards from the huge tree that held the tree house. It swayed to and fro gently but the man could tell there was a long trunk raised and checking the air for any scent that might indicate danger.

"Helene," called Ki-Gor softly, "our friend has arrived. See, there in the edge of the jungle? That dark spot that is moving slightly, that is Marmo. We should go down and meet him and I will tell him that we want to leave early tomorrow."

"Ki-Gor!" exclaimed Helene. "You know Marmo can't understand you. He just kind of pretends like he knows what you say to him."

"Helene," said her mate, "you have not lived in the jungle long enough yet. But the time will come when you will believe that many of the beasts understand what you are saying. It may be by the tone of your voice or by, what you call, body language. But they are a lot smarter than civilized man would give them credit for being!"

The woman smiled at her man. "Let's go down and say 'hello' to our friend, o' husband of mine!"

The rising sun the following morning found the great gray elephant moving along at a steady swaying pace. Perched on his neck just behind the large ears was Ki-Gor, bronzed lord of the jungle. Swaying on the shoulders and using a long leather band that was fastened around the beast, just behind the front legs and coming up over the back, was Helene. She had two large woven sacks that were tied together and slung over the shoulders of the great beast. She had plans to fill these with the pretty, rounded stones from the river.

At mid morning they came to a swiftly flowing stream of clear water. It was quite clear and appeared to be rather cool. Ki-Gor stopped the elephant and they dismounted to stretch and quench their thirst, even though there were water gourds among their supplies on the beast.

"This is good tasting water," said Helene after she had drank from the stream. "It is quite cool."

"It comes from that mountain range to the south."

"Let us walk for a little bit," said the woman. "I am somewhat stiff from riding. Maybe in half a mile I will be ready to ride some more."

Both Ki-Gor and Helene carried an assegai, the man's being somewhat larger than the woman's, and each had a large knife in a sheath belted about their waist.

They walked with long strides and a swinging gait that rapidly covered the ground and Marmo followed along directly behind them. Occasionally the huge beast would pull a clump of vegetation and stuff it in his mouth, eating as they walked. They traveled on foot for a good ten minutes and then remounted.

They continued their ride steadily toward the southeast. When they crossed a ridge an hour later, Ki-Gor pointed out to his companion the Shikashika Mountains in the distance.

"That is where the Ieka River comes from," he explained. "It is a good river and it winds extensively around the hills and through jungle patches. I might have been tempted to build our home in this area as it is very nice here. But we would be a little too close to the Salguba, cousins of the Wunguba, who were responsible for the death of my father." It was a long speech for Ki-Gor, even now, after spending so much time with Helene Vaughn and learning to speak correct English.

"There are people here who do not like you?" asked the girl. "Are we in any danger?"

"We are in danger only if the Salguba or Wunguba should discover we are here," he replied.

The small grass thatched hut stood at the north end of the Salguba village. It was not large and there was a distinctive odor emanating from it. The stench was so strong that even the young children, playing in the village, kept their distance. The only time anyone went there was when there was an ailment that would not go away on its own. Then the help of the sorcerer, living within the squalor, was needed.

T'Chuka came to the door of his hut and squinted in the bright sunlight. He leaned his near five-foot boney frame on his wooden staff, his stringy white hair fluffing in the slight breeze. For long moments he watched the children at play and they did not seem to notice him.

"Boy!" he finally called out, pointing at one of the youngsters, "Come here!" His voice was shrill and high pitched. The children stopped their play at the strange voice as they very rarely saw the old man and hardly ever heard him speak.

The youngster came quickly and stopped in front of the old man, his body trembling. His mouth opened but no sound came out.

"Boy!" came the raspy, but shrill voice. "Find your father and send him to me! Be quick now! If he does not come, I will turn him into a mouse! Hurry!"

The youngster, gasping slightly for a breath of clean air, turned and rushed away. The other children moved farther away from the old man's hut and resumed their game of kick-ball and it was obvious they did not let their ball of bound rags and skins get anywhere near the dwelling of the sorcerer.

A very short time later, M'Gutu arrived at the hut. T'Chuka had been watching for him and met him at the door.

"Come in," he said in a whisper. "There is a matter that I must discuss with you."

"I cannot," the man replied. "I am on duty near the far trail. We have cattle and goats there and I should not be absent. Only for you and our chief would I leave my duty! But I must hurry back before the lion or the jackals discover my absence. What is this matter of importance?"

"So be it," the old man replied, moving out into the sunlight and a little farther away from the rancid odor of his domicile. The reek of stale body sweat and the smell of rotted meat seemed to follow the old fellow.

T'Chuka leaned on his staff and looked upward, through bloodshot eyes, at the taller man. "I am at a time in life where I need the blood of a white man to fix a potion that will give me longer life. I charge you to find what I need. Should you not do this small task for me," the old fellow added, "I will turn all your children into mice. Then I will turn your woman into a cat!"

"How quickly must you have the body of a white man?" asked M'Gutu. Then he added, "This will be no easy task!"

"Um, no, no!" the sorcerer said. "Not a lifeless body! I must have warm blood! Bring the man to me alive and I will take his blood then!"

"As you wish," said the man, "but how soon is this required? It cannot be done overnight, as you full well know!"

"Um, perhaps a week will suffice," the old sorcerer nodded.

"I must find our chief and make arrangements for someone to replace me while I am on this journey," said M'Gutu. "Perhaps I can arrange for a warrior or two to accompany me."

Old T'Chuka nodded, then turned and plodded back into the darkness of his foul smelling abode. "I am still important," he muttered to himself with a slight grin on his nearly toothless mouth. "Yes, I can still make demands and expect them to be carried out!"

M'Gutu went directly to Chief Magawa's dwelling. There he tapped lightly on a door gong. Soon the Chief's daughter, Nene, was standing in front of the warrior.

"My father will see you now," she said softly but with a bright smile on her face. In his state of mind, M'Gutu did not notice. He was too concerned about the threats of the sorcerer.

"Sit," said Chief Magawa as M'Gutu entered his presence. "What brings you here at this time of day?"

The man related his story to his chief along with the threats that had been made by the old sorcerer. "I cannot take a chance that he will turn my children into mice!" he exclaimed.

The chief nodded in understanding. "I wonder how he knew," he muttered. Then he looked back at M'Gutu. "I have my doubts that he can turn anyone into anything at all!" he said. "I was a young man when he became our witch doctor or sorcerer. I have watched him for years and I do not know of any single incident where he really changed anyone into something else! I do not think you have any worries there, my friend!"

"But he might be able to do that and we would never know," said M'Gutu. "How many tribal members have we had that just disappeared in the jungle? Some every year, it seems. How do we know that it was not the old sorcerer changing them into some wild animal? Perhaps it was something that was slain by our hunters and brought back to our village for us to feed upon!"

"Hmm," nodded the chief. "That could be so. However, this thought has also crossed my mind. Were you aware there is a white man camped in the big bend of the river not half a day's journey from here?"

M'Gutu shook his head negatively. "No, I did not know," he said. "That would be a much easier task than trying to bring in the Jungle Lord! I am sure he meant for me to go after the big white man!"

"I knew about this white man," said the chief, "and the warrior who reported it to me would know. But there should be no others. I demanded he remain silent about this until I had time to reflect upon it. So how did T'Chuka know? No one gossips with him!"

"He is a sorcerer," said M'Gutu, as if that would explain everything. "He knows all."

"Did T'Chuka specifically tell you that you should bring in Ki-Gor for his blood?"

The warrior shook his head. "No, he just said that he needed the blood of a white man and that it had to be fresh, that is, come from a living being! So I have to bring in a white man that is still alive!"

"You are more likely to be successful if you go after that white man on the river. Pick two men and tell me who you are taking before you leave. When you return, I want to see the white man before you take him to the sorcerer."

"Will you assign someone as a lookout for the herd?" asked M'Gutu.

"Daughter," the chief called and when the girl appeared, he asked her to go stand watch with the herd until he had found a replacement for her. He assured her that she would not be out very long.

When the girl left the dwelling, she batted her eyes at M'Gutu who was leaving at the same time. This time the man noticed. He smiled at the girl and then turned, moving away to search for the two men he wanted to take with him to find the white man.

"Doesn't the girl know," he murmured to himself, "that I already have a woman and we have four children!" Still it felt good that a young woman was showing interest in him. He smiled as he hurried along.

Late in the afternoon, Ki-Gor turned to look back at Helene riding on Marmo's back. "The clouds say it will rain in a short while," he said. "Do you wish to find a dry place or should we continue on in the rain?"

"Will it be really heavy," the young woman asked. "If it is a light shower, I would just as soon keep going."

"One never knows for sure about the rain," the jungle man replied. "But I think it will not be a hard one. We will continue toward the river."

"How far away is the river?" asked Helene. "Are we getting close?"

"Yes, we are getting close," her husband replied. "You see that ridge over there? The one extending outward? The river flows around it and comes this way. We should be at the bend soon. There is a drop off on this side of about fifteen or twenty feet. We will look for a place where we can go down and cross the water. On the opposite side is a wide sandy area, maybe as much as two hundred to three hundred feet wide. Beyond that is jungle."

"George's scout said the white man was camped right on the sandy area, didn't he?"

Ki-Gor nodded. "Not a good place to pitch a tent," he replied. "If there were to be a heavy rain up in the mountains, he could be washed away before he knew it was coming."

"Are you going to warn him about the danger of his location?" asked Helene.

"Perhaps, if we actually talk to him. It depends on what kind of man he is. Many white men do not want someone like me making suggestions. To them I am still a wild savage and would not know anything!"

"You think we might not talk to this man?" asked the girl.

"We are here to determine what brings this fellow to our country," replied the bronzed giant. "If he does not seem to be a danger, we may just go on without actually going into his camp."

"Do you expect that to happen?"

"No, I do not," replied Ki-Gor with a light chuckle.

The rain began to fall. It was light at first, but then it became heavier and Helene shivered slightly. "This is colder than I had thought it would be," she commented.

"It is colder because of the mountains. Do you wish to find shelter?" the man asked.

"No. I am more anxious to find this bend in the river and see just what it is that we have made this long elephant ride to check out!"

"We'll be there in a few minutes," her companion replied.

True to his word, they were soon approaching an open space in the jungle. The elephant stopped as Ki-Gor spoke to him. Then he reached up and lifted the man to the ground. This was followed by Helene being placed beside him.

"Is this the bluff we are to see the camp from?" asked Helene.

"Yes," nodded Ki-Gor. "You can't tell it because of the falling rain and when we get to the edge, we may not be able to see much."

"Perhaps we should have stayed on Marmo," suggested the young woman.

"No," the man replied. "Marmo shouldn't get too close because he weighs close to ten tons and he could cause the cliff wall to crumble. That is not the way we want to get down to the river level."

"Speaking of how big our friend, Marmo, is," said Helene, "just how tall do you think he is? I know I am a long ways up in the air when we are riding him!"

"I believe his is between fourteen and fifteen feet at the shoulder," Ki-Gor replied. "And his tusks are at least eight feet in length! He is a big boy!"

"Is he the largest elephant you have ever seen?" asked the redhead.

"No," replied Ki-Gor, "but he is right up there. Not many are larger than Marmo!"

Ki-Gor spoke to the elephant and he turned to enter the sparse jungle where he could feed.

The man and woman moved to the edge of the cliffs and sprawled out on the wet ground where they would not be so visible from the camp below them. The rain was still falling.

...followed by Helene being placed beside Ki-Gor.

"I don't see anything going on down there," said Helene after they had watched for a short time.

Ki-Gor laughed softly. "You are from the tribe of white Americans," he said. "Your people are always in a hurry. Sometimes it is best to wait and watch. The patient hunter is often rewarded."

"Like right now," said Helene, "I am stretched out here in the falling rain watching... nothing!"

Ki-Gor raised his arm and placed it across the narrow shoulders of the girl snuggled close beside him.

"Your arm is warm," said his companion. "I feel better already," she added with a mischievous grin.

"Look," said Ki-Gor softly, nodding toward the clearing across the river.

At first the girl could see nothing. The rain was beginning to slacken, but the area was still somewhat foggy. Then she gave a short gasp as she had picked out what Ki-Gor had seen.

A dark shadow had detached itself from the jungle undergrowth and was moving across the clearing toward the lone tent that was pitched there. As they watched, the native stopped a few paces from the canvas dwelling. They could not hear him, but from his body action, they were sure he had called out to someone within. Presently a flap was pushed back and a tall lean man stepped out into the now lightly falling rain.

It appeared the two were conversing for a few moments and then without warning, the man raised a walking stick and struck the black man across the side of the neck with a sharp stunning blow! The fellow dropped to his knees, grasping at his neck. Then his hands fell away and his body slumped backwards in an awkward position.

"I think he just killed that man," said Ki-Gor. "We must keep a close watch on him when we go to talk to him."

"When will we go to see him?" asked Helene. "He's not in a very good mood right now."

"By the time we find Marmo, locate a slope he can descend and then cross the river," said Ki-Gor, "the white man will have had some time to gather himself together. It would be interesting to know what caused him to strike that blow."

"Does Marmo need to go with us?" asked Helene. "If that fellow is a big game hunter, he may decide he has to bring Marmo down as his big game trophy!"

"I do not understand that," said Ki-Gor, "to kill something just because it is big! However, we need Marmo to carry us across the river. It has some deep spots and is quite wide. Do you think you could swim that?"

"Maybe," said the girl, "if I was forced to. But I'd much rather ride Marmo."

The elephant was feeding and not too far from the spot where Ki-Gor and Helene had dismounted. At the man's whistle, which was not nearly as loud or as sharp as some that the girl had heard her husband issue, the big pachyderm was soon coming toward them from the jungle. The man went to meet him, reaching up and caressing the animal's cheek while the huge trunk moved softly over his friend's body. Then the redheaded woman stepped up beside the man and the elephant recognized her as well.

In minutes the great beast had placed both Ki-Gor and Helene on his neck and back respectively and they were moving along the lip of the cliff, but maintaining enough distance to feel safe with the elephant's great weight. They found two crumbling slopes not far from where they had earlier dismounted, but neither slope appeared safe or stable enough for the fellow to attempt descending. But the third time they located a slope, it seemed perfect and Marmo began picking his way carefully downward.

The descent was made without incident and they were soon on the riverbank which was about a thirty yard sand bank between the cliff and the water's edge. They were about three hundred yards downstream from the point where the white man had set up his camp.

Marmo had no trouble getting across the moving water and soon Ki-Gor and Helene were dismounting on the opposite side of the river. The man patted the beast and told him to go and find food while he was in the camp of the white man. Whether the elephant actually understood the man or not, is debatable. Elephants are quite intelligent and this one had been around Ki-Gor for a long period of time. As the pachyderm was leaving, the man warned him to be on the lookout for hunters. A light whuffing sound came from the trunk and the man grinned.

The elephant went in the direction away from the campsite, while Ki-Gor and his mate made their way in the opposite direction, toward the camp. Soon they were standing at the edge of the jungle looking toward the camp. The body of the black man still lay where it had fallen; however, there was now a light on in the tent.

The jungle man and his mate approached the tent and, following the procedure of the downed black man, they stopped some distance away.

"White man!" came the bronze giant's deep authoritative voice, "Ki-Gor, Lord of the Jungle, would have words with you!"

"Um," said Helene, giving a little shiver, "that almost sounded confrontational!"

That was not a word Ki-Gor would have used, but from the context of its use, he knew what it meant. He smiled at Helene. Everyday he was learning more and more concerning the English language.

The tent flap moved slightly and a man's face peeked out. Then seeing only a well developed young man in a leopard skin and a beautiful young woman standing beside him, neither of which carried modern weapons, the fellow stepped out of his tent. He looked somewhat uncertain as he came forward. Ki-Gor and Helene remained standing about the same distance away from the tent as the downed, inert body of the native; however, they were several feet to one side.

"Hello," said the man, offering his right hand for a handshake, but then seeing that Ki-Gor held a huge assegai in his right hand, the man dropped his hand. Helene saw the attempt of a handshake but assumed her husband probably did not recognize it for what it was.

"My name is Gabriel Jacobson," the man continued. "Just call me Gabe and welcome to my camp. What can I do for you?"

"To begin with," said Ki-Gor, in a calm friendly voice, "we would like to know what you are doing in this part of the jungle? Are you hunting? Are you looking to gather slaves? Are you wanting to claim land for farming? I am Ki-Gor, Lord of the Jungle and I would like to know these things."

"Ki-Gor!" exclaimed the white man, "I have heard the natives speak of you, but I assumed you were just another one of their stories. They tell so many, you know. Usually in an attempt to not have to do what is required of them!"

"Mr. Jacobson," said Helene, smiling sweetly, "I am Helene. Ki-Gor is my husband and we come in friendship, although we are concerned as to what motive brings you here?"

"You speak American English!" the man exclaimed. "That is music to my ears! What part of America are you from?"

"New England," the girl replied, not giving the man a definite answer.

"I'm from Oklahoma," the man replied. "I'm in oil, you know."

"What brings you to this part of Africa's jungles?" asked Ki-Gor.

The man gave a wry smile. "None of the reasons you just mentioned," he said. "I brought my two boys with me and we came basically for a vacation and for the experience of living and traveling in a strange locale. I thought it would do them some good, you know."

"How old are the boys?" asked Helene.

"Youngest one is ten," the man said. "The oldest one is twelve, pushing thirteen."

"Quite young," replied the woman. "Where are they now?"

"Oh, they are around here somewhere," Jacobson replied. "They've been having a ball playing on this sandy beach. Really a good place for setting up camp, if I do say so myself."

"Did your native bearers try to persuade you not to camp right here?" asked Helene.

"Well, yeah, they did," the man replied, giving the redheaded woman a sharp look. "How did you know?"

"This is a very poor place to camp," said Ki-Gor. "You have set yourself up to be washed away should there be a heavy rain in the mountains. By the time you realized the water was coming, you would not have time to get out of the path. That would be a terrible way to lose your sons!"

"How long has it been since you've seen your boys?" asked Helene.

"Oh, twenty or thirty minutes," Gabe Jacobson replied.

"Have you been sleeping?" asked Ki-Gor.

"Well, yes, I was taking a little nap. Then that fellow, Bob, came back and began to harangue me about moving the camp. He also said that Joe and Bill had disappeared and that he could not find them."

"Would Joe and Bill be your sons?" asked Helene, a worried look on her face.

"No, no," the man said, wiping his face. "Joe and Bill were the remaining two askari members. All the rest have gradually sneaked out and gone back to their villages! At least, I guess that is where they went! You can't depend on these buggers at all!"

"These natives were named Bob, Joe and Bill?" asked Ki-Gor. "That is strange. I've never heard of those names being used by the natives."

Jacobson shook his head. "No, they had some other type of tom-foolery name! Hard to pronounce so I just changed them while they were working for me."

"You gave everybody you hired to work for you new names?" asked Helene, a tone of disbelief in her voice."

"Yeah, it was better that way," Jacobson said.

"What are the names of your sons?" the woman asked.

"Jerold and Raymond," the man responded. "Named for a couple of their uncles. They just go by Jerry and Ray."

"What happened to the fellow there in the sand?" asked Ki-Gor.

Jacobson hesitated and then said, "The guy jumped me when he came back and I had to club him with my walking stick. I thought he'd be up and around by now."

"Mr. Jacobson," said Helene, "I hate to dispute your word, but we've been watching your camp for over an hour now and while we haven't had it under surveillance every minute, we have seen most of what has gone on here. In all this time, we have not seen any sign of your two boys. We also saw the man in the sand, Bob, I believe you called him, and he did not attack you. We are wondering why you hit him?"

"Were you trying to kill him?" asked Ki-Gor, a hard tone in his voice.

Gabe Jacobson got a stunned look on his face. "He ain't dead!" he finally exclaimed. "I never killed a man in my life!"

"He sure looks dead," said Ki-Gor, turning and walking over to the man Gabe Jacobson had renamed Bob. As he bent over the downed man, he heard a squeal and felt the strong slap of the walking stick come down over his back. The stick broke.

Ki-Gor gave a roar and whirled toward the white man. At the same time Helene's smaller assegai was thrust against the fellow's chest and she began to push him backwards.

Jacobson fumbled at the handgun holstered on his belt. By the time he got the weapon out, Ki-Gor's large hand clasped his gun hand in a crushing grip that brought a howl of pain from the man.

The jungle man lifted the American by the hand and then slammed him to the ground beside the native the fellow had felled earlier. The breath was knocked from the man and he laid gasping and kicking in the sand.

At that moment the native, Bob, suddenly gave a gasp and sat up. Helene reached down and took the man's hand, then helped pull him to his feet. He was somewhat woozy, but he managed to stand.

Ki-Gor turned and handed the pistol to Helene and as he was doing so, Gabe Jacobson rolled over and then sprang to his feet.

"Nobody treats me that way," he snarled as he charged into the jungle man, his fists swinging.

Ki-Gor took a step backwards and then planted a strong cuff on the side of the man's head. The man gave a grunt and sat down on the ground again, his head spinning.

"How many times do you have to get knocked down before you learn?" asked Helene in a very kind voice. "It doesn't have to be this way."

"If you really had a couple of boys," said Ki-Gor, "I would think you would be more concerned about their safety!"

Helene turned to Bob who was rubbing the side of his neck. "Does this man have two sons out here in the jungle somewhere?" she asked.

"Yes, he does," the native replied. "The boys are just as foolish as the father," he added.

"Where are they?"

The native shrugged. "They can be anywhere and do anything they want," he said. "That is the decision of the father."

Ki-Gor reached down and caught Gabe Jacobson by the front of his shirt and lifted him upright. The man's eyes were glinting in anger. The jungle man raised Gabe off his feet before he spoke.

"If you attempt to hit me again, white man, I will see if I can knock your head completely off your shoulders! Do you understand me?"

Gabe Jacobson nodded. Ki-Gor sat him back on the ground.

"We need to get this man's camp back away from the river on higher ground," he said. "I do not know that it rained hard in the mountains, but I would not be surprised. Once the camp is moved, we need to find the boys. Jacobson, take your tent down and box everything. We are moving you to higher ground."

"Are there any other members of this man's safari left?" asked Helene.

"Joe and Bill may not be too far away," replied the native. "They took shelter during the rain. They might come back if the foolish one is no longer in command. Otherwise, they are going on home."

"What is your real name, Bob?" asked Helene.

"Katonga," the man replied. "I am called Katonga. Joe and Bill are Wumba and Natil. If we call them by their real names, they might come back and help," the man grinned.

A distant rumble of thunder came from the mountains. Ki-Gor and Katonga both looked toward the mountain range.

"Is it raining up there?" asked Helene.

Ki-Gor shrugged. "Maybe," he replied.

It did not take long to dismantle the tent. Soon they were moving the equipment back from the open area near the running water.

"There is a meadow in that direction," said Katonga. "Not far from here. We tried to get the white man to set his camp up there, but he refused."

Ki-Gor nodded. "We'll place him there now."

"Gabe Jacobson," said Ki-Gor, once they had moved all the camping gear up the slope, "do you have any idea where your two sons are? You have been here several days. Perhaps they have a favorite place where they spend time?"

"I don't know," the man grumbled, still miffed that he had been moved away from the river. "The natives keep telling me about all the dangers out here in the jungles. But I've not seen anything that backs up their stories! I haven't seen a large animal since we left the coast!"

"The large animals are here," said Helene gently. "You don't see them because they see you first. They have no desire to cross paths with you. Only if they were hungry would certain ones stalk you."

The white man just glared at Helene. "You dumb natives are always trying to scare me!" he growled, glancing at all three of the individuals who had moved his camp.

"Perhaps," said Ki-Gor, "if we can find the remains of your sons, you will change your mind!"

"Do you believe Wumba and Natil are still where they took shelter from the rain?" asked Helene.

"They had started a fire and were preparing to eat," said Katonga.

"Would you be willing to go see if you can convince them to return?"

Katonga nodded.

"We will look for Jerry and Ray while you are gone," she added.

"Do you have any idea where your sons may be?" asked Ki-Gor, turning to the white man. "We should be finding them as quickly as we can. Those beasts you cannot see are out there!"

Gabe Jacobson opened his mouth to say something when a faint scream floated across the damp breeze. The white man thought it was a monkey up in the trees.

Ki-Gor whirled and pointed. "That way!" he said and left the area at a dead run. Helene was close on his heels.

"They are crazy," Jacobson muttered to himself. "If there were any big animals around, I would certainly have seen them."

Rummaging through his supplies, Jacobson produced another pistol which he placed in the holster on his belt. He saw the heavy duty rifle he had brought along in case he wanted to do a little hunting for sport. He frowned in disgust.

"I can't believe I fell for all those stories about big, dangerous, exotic animals here in Africa!" he exploded. "There is nothing on this continent but heat and dirt! When the boys come back, we're going to head for the coast and catch the first ship back to Oklahoma!"

Gabe Jacobson managed to get a small fire going and was sitting beside it when Katonga stepped out of the jungle with Wumba and Natil just behind him. He walked toward the white man.

"The boys are back," he said, indicating the two men with him.

"It's about time," the man grumbled.

"They will work for you, to get you back to the coast. You must call them by their right names," Katonga added. "You must let them do the work as they see fit. The way Ki-Gor would have them do it."

Jacobson frowned. "What does Ki-Gor have to do with it? He ain't running this show!"

Katonga looked at Jacobson, his face impassive. "You have managed to run off all the boys who started out with you," he said. "If you want any help getting out of here, you must treat Wumba and Natil with a little more respect!"

"I know you have had some schooling, Katonga," the man said, standing up, "but that doesn't mean you know anything! You're nothing more than a dumb native! This is my safari and I will run it the way I see fit!"

Wumba and Natil looked at each other. "We leave," one of them said.

"No, wait," pleaded Katonga. "Ki-Gor will return and we can get this all straightened out. It will take Bwana Jacobson some time to change, but we can get him back to the coast. Then we can be paid for our work! Otherwise, we have made nothing!"

"Um," grunted Wumba. "Where little boys?"

"Out playing in the jungle," replied Katonga. "Ki-Gor is out looking for them, I think."

"Bad," said Wumba. "No good."

"Put up the tent for Bwana Jacobson," suggested Katonga. "I shall go help look for the boys. It will be dark before long. They should have been back by now."

Gabe Jacobson gave Katonga a glaring look. "Jerry and Ray can take care of themselves," he said. "They are not dumb, like you bearers!"

Katonga turned and entered the jungle while Wumba and Natil began putting the camp in order. As they worked darkness fell. Gabe Jacobson sat on a stool, watched and pouted.

Ki-Gor and Helene came to a rocky knoll that was somewhat devoid of heavy vegetation. On the ground they found a handful of flowers that someone had picked.

"One of the boys was making a bouquet to take back to the camp," said Helene softly. "I wonder why he dropped them?"

"Here," said Ki-Gor suddenly. "This is blood on the rock! If he fell and hurt himself, that may have been the scream we heard."

The jungle man dropped to his knees and lowered his head close to the ground, sniffing of the area around the spot where they had found droplets of blood.

"Here," he said, motioning for Helene. "You smell, too. This is something like stale water in a swamp. It should not be up here."

Helene dropped to the ground and tried to pick up the odor that Ki-Gor had found. It took a little time, but she finally caught a vague scent that did remind her of swamp water.

"I can smell it," she said. "I'm getting better at this!"

"Yes, you are," Ki-Gor smiled. "The trail is too faint to follow in the dark and I need light to see other markings."

"Let's return to the camp," said Helene. "Surely Jacobson has a flashlight we can use. Those little boys are out there somewhere and I'll bet they are just scared to pieces!"

"Yes," Ki-Gor nodded.

They stood up just as Katonga came out of the jungle, some twenty yards away and immediately trotted toward them.

"Have you found any trace of the boys?" he asked. "It is getting dark and soon the beasts will be prowling, looking for food. We need to find them. They are like their father. They do not know enough to be afraid."

"We have found where they were a short while ago," replied Ki-Gor. "Come and tell me what you smell here on the ground."

"One of the boys hurt himself and there is a little blood on a rock," said Helene. "It will draw meat eaters before long."

Katonga came forward; saw the smudge of blood on the stone, then knelt to the ground to see what scent he could pick up. Almost immediately he was back on his feet, his eyes large.

"Whew!" he said, passing his hand in front of his nose, as though to brush the smell away. "I have not caught that scent in a long time," he said in a quavering voice.

"What is it?" asked Ki-Gor.

"Have you seen or heard of a small flying creature called a Gyjak. It resembles a lizard with wings and it smells like that," Katonga said.

"I have heard of the flying lizard," nodded Ki-Gor, "but did not actually believe it was a real thing."

"You referred to it as being small," said Helene. "Just how small is it?"

"The body is about this long," said the native measuring out about a foot with his hands. "Each wing is about that long as well. He has a wing spread about this wide," and he measured out about two feet with his hands.

"How dangerous are they?" asked Helene. "Are they poisonous?"

"I don't know," said Katonga. "I have only seen one and it was not up close. I think they are very rare and I don't think anyone knows if they carry a poison or not. Also, no one knows how big they might get. What I saw may have been a very young one."

Ki-Gor and Helene were both nodding.

"Is the scent strong enough for you to follow in the dark?" asked the jungle man.

"No," said the native. "I have been in civilization too much. It dulls your senses."

"Katonga," said Helene, "you speak like an educated man. Have you had some schooling?"

The fellow grinned at that and nodded. "Yes," he said. "I attended school back on the coast off and on for several years. Enough to learn to speak good English!"

"It shows," smiled Helene.

"I think there is a flying lizard, a Gyjak, out there with those two boys," said Ki-Gor. "How much danger are they in?"

Katonga shrugged his shoulders. "I don't know," he said, shaking his head.

"Let's go back to the camp," said Helene, "and see if this Gabe fellow has a flashlight. We might be able to find the boys that way."

With Katonga leading, they immediately broke into a ground covering pace for the camp. When they arrived, Wumba and Natil had the big tent up and were arranging items about the campsite.

Helene went immediately to Gabe Jacobson, who was seated on a camp stool near the entrance to his tent smoking his pipe.

"We have found where the boys were," she said. "We are wondering if you would have a flashlight so that we might try to follow their trail."

"It is dark now," said the man. "They'll be in pretty soon."

"There was blood on a rock," said Helene. "One of the boys may have suffered an injury. We would like to find them as quickly as possible."

In the distance came the cough of a hunting lion. The sound had just died away when the night was filled with a loud cackling sound from the opposite direction.

"Did you hear those cries in the jungle?" asked Helene. "Those are predators who would not hesitate to make a meal of your children, Gabe Jacobson! Now, do you have a flashlight?"

The man rose, went into his tent and came back with a flashlight, which he handed to Helene.

"Thank you," she said, taking the flashlight. Immediately she pressed the

"I attended school back on the coast..."

button to turn it on. There was a very dull light emanating from it.

"Do you have more batteries?" she asked.

"Did have," the fellow said, nonchalantly. "But we used them up."

"So you really don't have a light, do you?"

"Nope," grinned Jacobson.

Helene turned to Ki-Gor. "Would torches help?" she asked.

The man shook his head. "Not enough light. Also, a torch flickers causing you to see movement that is not there."

"What are we going to do?" asked Helene.

There was a movement in the brush at the edge of the clearing and Ki-Gor saw it.

"There is something there," he said in a soft voice. "Perhaps it is the boys."

"Jerry! Ray! Come on in, boys," called Gabe Jacobson, who had heard Ki-Gor's comment to Helene. "About time you kids got back! These strangers won't hurt you!"

There was no response from the shadows where there had been movement. Ki-Gor placed both hands on his assegai, holding it in front of him, and moved toward the jungle. Helene was right behind and to one side of him, holding her smaller assegai in a similar position.

Gabe Jacobson watched them moving silently away from him and noticed that Helene still had his hand gun stuck under her belt. He grunted and thought he would have to find a way to get the gun back.

With no sound, a figure emerged from the jungle growth. The person was tall and dark, blending well with the shadows. One hand was upraised, bringing both Ki-Gor and Helene to a stop. Katonga stepped up by the jungle man with his hand raised in response to the visitor.

The tall figure, wearing a loin cloth and wide belt also sported a number of necklaces made of small bones, claws and other items, including pieces of cloth.

The first words from the stranger's mouth were high pitched and soft, almost musical. It was a dialect that neither Ki-Gor nor Helene could place. However, Katonga answered, but his reply did not carry the beauty of the visitor's voice.

As they spoke, a leopard emerged from the shadows and sat at the feet of the tall figure. The beast licked his paw and then wiped the side of his face, seemingly uninterested in those around him.

The conversation lasted less than a minute. Then the leopard disappeared into the jungle and a few seconds later, the tall visitor was gone as well. As the figure turned to leave, they saw a small form drop from an overhanging branch and light on the shoulder of the departing visitor.

Katonga turned to Ki-Gor and Helene. "Let us go back to Jacobson and I will tell you what she had to say."

"She?" asked Ki-Gor. "That was a female?"

Katonga nodded. "Had she come farther into the firelight, I think you could have seen that she was."

"I had a feeling she was a female," said Helene. "She was just too pretty to be a warrior!"

"Huh," Ki-Gor grunted. He hadn't noticed that she was pretty.

"What was that all about?" asked Jacobson, as they approached. He stood by the flap of his tent, a high powered rifle in his hands.

"That was Meca Huko," said Katonga. "In her language, it means Lightning Woman or Woman of Storms. She was aware that we had been out looking for the two boys. She brought us information concerning them."

"Well, where are my boys?" demanded Jacobson, a glowering look on his face.

"One was injured," said Katonga softly. "It was by something poisonous and he was taken so that a remedy could be applied. I believe they intend to bring him back in the morning, assuming they have counteracted the poison."

"Which one?" snapped Jacobson.

"I believe she said it was the larger of the two. That would be Jerry."

"Where is Ray? Why didn't she bring him back?"

"She didn't say," replied Katonga. "Perhaps he wanted to stay with his brother."

"Get the boys," Jacobson barked, referring to Wumba and Natil. "We're gonna follow that fellow and see where the kids are! I want them back here! Now!"

"If one boy got into some poison," said Helene, "perhaps both of them did."

"I think it was more of an injury," said Katonga, "like a bite, perhaps."

"You think a snake bit him?" asked Jacobson.

Katonga shrugged. "Perhaps," he said. "It might have been a monkey or something, especially if they had been teasing it."

"Let's get going! Time's wasting! We've got to get after that guy!"

"That guy was a gal," said Helene. "And I doubt that there is any kind of trail. She seemed like an entity that would not leave a trail."

"What do you mean by that?" snapped the man.

"She was light on her feet," said Helene. "She had a leopard with her and as she left, I believe that was a monkey that dropped down on her shoulder. Ki-Gor might be able to pick up her trail but I wouldn't be surprised if there was nothing there."

"Balderdash!" fumed the man. "Get those lazy bearers and let's get out there and find my sons!"

"Too bad you didn't check on them when you had daylight," said Ki-Gor calmly. "It would have been much easier to find them."

Gabe Jacobson glared at the big jungle man. He so badly wanted to put that fellow in his place! Teach him a lesson!

Thunder rumbled and a light rain began to fall. Had there been any trail to follow, Mother Nature had taken care of eliminating it.

Ki-Gor and Helene moved toward the spot where the tall woman had stood. When they got there, they picked up a faint scent of a Gyjak, but that soon faded with the falling rain.

"Katonga," said Ki-Gor when that man and the two bearers arrived, "I thought I could scent a Gyjak, like up in the rocks earlier. Can you pick up the scent?"

"Don't have to," the man replied. "I saw the critter drop onto Meca Huko's shoulder as she left. I assume you know there will be no trail to follow," he added. "She just won't leave one."

"So that was a flying lizard and not a monkey," exclaimed Helene. "It sure looked like a monkey."

"He had his wings folded," said Katonga. "He just dropped a couple of feet, so he didn't need to spread his wings. And those two boys were throwing rocks at a Gyjak. I believe Meca Huko indicated both boys had been bitten, but I'm not sure. She was speaking an ancient dialect used many generations back, so I am not actually sure about that."

"She did say she would bring the boys back in the morning, didn't she?" asked Helene.

"I think that is what she said," replied Katonga. "She may have said they should be well in the morning. I had a feeling she wasn't going to return them herself, but rather just turn them out to find their own way back."

"Do you know where she might have taken them?" asked Ki-Gor.

"Let us move into the jungle and out of sight of Bwana Jacobson," said Katonga as he saw that man emerge from his tent.

Katonga led the four individuals with him deeper into the jungle. They had covered about fifty yards when he came to a stop. They were under a huge tree that sheltered them from the falling rain.

"Bwana Jacobson will not come this far before he returns to his tent,"

Katonga explained. "As long as he feels he has someone out looking for his sons, he won't feel he needs to be out himself."

"No wonder everyone left him," said Helene. "Why did you stay, Katongo?"

"I feel somewhat responsible for the man," he replied. "I helped him put his safari together and that makes me feel like I should take care of him and his sons. Had I known what kind of fellow he would turn out to be, I would have never agreed to help him.

"Back to your question, Ki-Gor," said Katonga, "I do not know where Meca Huko, or someone else, would have taken the boys. I do not know of any villages in this area. The lack of people is part of the reason we are in this particular location."

"So where will they put the boys when they release them?" asked Helene.

"I think in the area where they were teasing the Gyjaks," said the man.

"There was more than one?" she asked.

Katonga nodded. "At least two, but perhaps more."

"I thought they were rare," Helene replied.

"They are," said Katonga. "Somewhere in this region, and I do not know how close, there is said to be a burial cavern where royalty was buried. This was many generations ago. I'm going to guess at least a hundred and fifty years ago, perhaps more. At that time there were guardians of the caverns. It is my opinion Meca Huko is descended from them."

"There must be a village somewhere, then," said Helene.

Katonga nodded with a grim-lipped smile. "They have to be somewhere," he agreed.

"They have the Gyjaks," added Ki-Gor. "Why?"

"Perhaps they are just pets," suggested his mate.

"I believe they had something to do with maintaining the burial caverns," said Katonga, "but I do not know just what. The stories I have heard, long ago from elders, indicated there was something about the caverns that preserved the deceased. They did not decompose. They just remained as they were when they passed away. Much wealth was placed in the caverns with the deceased because the living thought they would eventually come back to life and they would need the wealth to maintain the life style they were accustomed to in their previous life. Because of that, there are many who have tried to find these burial chambers. To my knowledge, no one has ever found them or even been close. You see, the Gyjaks were connected with the guardians and no one has ever seen one that I am aware of, other then myself. But many may have been seen, as it is not something that would make big news."

"You say they stopped placing the deceased in the tombs or caverns a long time ago?" asked Helene. "I wonder why?"

"Long ago, they were known as the Smoking Caverns," said Katonga, "and you could see the smoke coming out of them. They were not hidden then, because it was easy to locate them. Plus, they were still being used. Then for some reason, the smoke stopped coming out of them. And since only royalty were placed there, they were not used too often. After tribal wars and villages moving, the location of the tomb was lost. Now, it is mostly just legend."

"I wonder if the smoke or fumes had something to do with the preservation of the bodies?" asked Helene.

"It would seem likely," agreed Katonga. "Our best chance of finding the location of those caverns would have been to follow Meca Huko. But I doubt we see her again."

"It would be a waste of time to try to find a trail in the dark and the rain," said Ki-Gor. "We need a good night's rest and then start fresh in the morning. If the rain has stopped, we can go back to the rock mound and see if the boys are brought to that spot."

"Where are we going to spend the night?" asked Helene.

"We'll find a protected dry spot here in the jungle somewhere," said Ki-Gor. "I do not trust Gabe Jacobson. But I shall go in and tell him that we are not out there looking in the rain. I will go by myself so the rest of you are not having to put up with his fits of temper."

"That will give him something else to worry about tonight," said Helene.

"I will go with Wumba and Natil," said Katonga. "They have a dry spot."

"Good," said Ki-Gor and raised a hand to the three departing men.

"We will look for a protected place as we return to the camp of Jacobson," said Ki-Gor.

It was not long before they found an uprooted tree that formed a nice dry spot and Helene was soon under it. Ki-Gor went on to the camp to let Jacobson know they had called off the search until daylight. Presently he was back.

"Did you talk to Jacobson?" Helene asked.

"No," said Ki-Gor. "When I got there, he was sound asleep. I did not wake him."

The following morning found Ki-Gor and Helene at the rocky knoll where they had found the blood spill the previous day. There was no sign of it now as the rain had washed the area clean.

"Do you think they will return the boys to this spot?" asked Helene.

Ki-Gor shrugged. "Maybe."

"But you don't think so, do you?"

"No."

Ki-Gor moved about fifty yards out from the rocky mound and made a complete circle of the area, but he found nothing. Then he moved out another fifty yards and did the same thing. This time he came upon a very faint trail that looked like something a small animal might follow. He finished his circuit, and finding nothing more, he returned to the trail and began to follow it. It wound about haphazardly and then came out in an open area close to a steep rocky slope. Here he found another trail that looked a little more promising.

The trail moved over to the slope and then just faded away. Ki-Gor looked at it and then studied the slope.

"I think," he said to Helene in a low voice, "that this trail, or another one, goes up the side of that rise. Let's see if we can work our way up to the top of the ridge."

There was a pathway but it was very sporadic. They worked their way along until they were some twenty feet above the base where they had started. Ki-Gor stopped and began looking over the area where they had recently been.

"Do you think someone may be following us?" Helene asked.

"I would not be surprised," Ki-Gor replied. "It is good to check your back trail."

While the Jungle Lord was looking over the area below them, checking for any kind of movement that seemed out of the ordinary, his mate was looking at the slope ahead and above them. Suddenly, she put her hand on his shoulder.

"Look up!" she whispered. "Above us!"

Ki-Gor quickly looked up and there, perched on a rock some thirty yards away was a Gyjak. He was just sitting in the morning sun gazing curiously at them.

"We must be getting close to something," Ki-Gor whispered, glancing at Helene who smiled at him. When the two looked back, the Gyjak was nowhere to be seen.

"How could he disappear so quickly?" the young woman asked.

"Animals do that," the blonde warrior replied. "He may have flown down below us and if we weren't looking at him when he did it, we very likely would not have seen him."

Helene nodded.

"We'll keep a watch for him as we continue upward," said Ki-Gor. "This is a very good sized slope and there could be all kinds of things concealed among the boulders and brush."

They continued upward and in a few minutes they were near where they had seen the flying lizard. They looked about them carefully, but the rock the creature had been sitting on was in a difficult spot to get to.

"We will go to the top," said Ki-Gor. "Perhaps we will see something from there."

They continued upward and after long minutes of climbing they reached the summit. They sat down to rest for a few minutes.

"I believe that is the rock right down there that the Gyjak was sitting on," Ki-Gor said. "I had thought it might be easier to get to that spot by climbing down, but there is a lot of brush in the way. I think I will go back down and see if I can get to that spot from the trail. You may stay here if you would like. I may have to do some crawling to get there."

"No," said Helene quickly. "I am going with you!"

Together they worked their way back down the trail and when they were even with the boulder where they had seen the flying lizard, the jungle man began working his way across and up the slope to reach it. Helene was right behind him. They did, indeed, do some crawling and by the time they reached the boulder, they were covered with dust and dirt. They also had a few minor scratches.

But the effort was worth it. Right behind the boulder they found a small hole leading back into the side of the hill.

"I could crawl in there," suggested Helene.

"Wait," Ki-Gor said studying the hole. "I think if I pushed this rock right here, it would roll away and then if I moved that one right there, the entrance would be large enough that I could get inside, too. Of course, it may just be a little cave that goes nowhere. But I think we need to check it out. And I don't want you going in until I have the hole large enough that I can get in there with you."

Helene smiled at her husband and he immediately began working on the two rocks he thought he could move. To his surprise, they moved very easily. Both moved inward when he began working on them.

"I think these were intended to be moved," he said. "Perhaps we could tell if they had been moved recently if it had not rained last night and yesterday."

Ki-Gor went first and Helene followed him. Once inside, they had to step down from a ledge that left them about chest high to the opening. They could easily stand upright and the cavern led deeper into the hill. Also, stacked near the opening, were a number of torches. Some had actually been used, while others had never been lit.

"Those big rocks you moved," said Helene, "just kind of slid inward on the shelf. It looks to me like that is what they were supposed to do. And with them out of the way, the opening lets in a lot of light."

"I know what you are thinking," said Ki-Gor with a grin. "You are thinking we should replace the stones so that it is not too obvious that someone came in here. That would be a smart move," and the jungle man went about replacing the big stones. "These move so easily, I believe they are hollowed out somewhat. Whoever did that, put in a lot of work!"

As Ki-Gor jostled the small boulders back into place, Helene took some matches from her belt pouch and lit one of the torches. It caught easily and burned brightly.

The man held the burning torch up high as they began their journey back into the cavern. His mate picked up extra unlit torches for when the time came that the first one was nearly burned out. They walked slowly, trying to observe everything as they went deeper into the darkness.

"Ki-Gor, there are cracks in the floor," said Helene. "I hope there aren't any spiders or snakes in them!"

"I think this tunnel was man made," said Ki-Gor quietly. "Or perhaps the walls and floor were just smoothed out after it was discovered."

"We seem to be going downhill," Helene added.

"We are either coming to the end or there is a sharp turn ahead of us."

In a few moments, they made a right hand turn and shortly thereafter, they came to an open doorway, also on their right hand side. Ki-Gor held the torch high and leaned it inside the room. His companion gave a squeal of fright!

Facing them were numerous figures in the dark room. Ki-Gor moved his assegai in front of him as he slowly entered the room with the flickering light of the torch. Circling the room were various stone seats with arm rests and backs. On each one was placed the dried remains of a human being. Most were draped with what had been at one time very opulent garments. Now they were decayed and dust covered and falling apart. Near the stone seats, or thrones, were various items that appeared to be made of precious metals and studded with various types of jewels.

"Do not touch anything," whispered Ki-Gor. "We don't want to leave any sign that we were here! Everything must remain exactly as it is now."

"This is mind boggling!" exclaimed Helene, also in a whisper.

"A light breeze would probably cause the remains of these people to crumble into a pile of dust," he added, "and I certainly do not want to be the cause of that!"

Ki-Gor and Helene looked about the room for a few minutes and then very quietly left. They had not moved far down the hallway when they saw another open doorway. A quick glance with the torch showed them another room containing the dried remains of long dead people. They did not enter this room, but continued onward.

The couple passed several rooms that were empty, as though they had never been used. But there were others that contained the ancient remains. They had walked past perhaps a dozen doorways when Helene touched Ki-Gor's arm.

"Have you noticed a faint odor?" she asked. "It is not very strong, but I think it smells like the Gyjak."

"Yes," nodded Ki-Gor. "I could smell it back at the entrance. Not very strong and I thought perhaps the little creature had passed through here."

"We haven't seen any sign of him," Helene agreed, "but it is pretty dark. He could be about anywhere and be hidden from us."

"Have you been aware of the gas coming up through the cracks in the floor?" asked Ki-Gor. "You can see it if you watch for it. I think it is getting thicker the farther we go."

"I see it now," nodded the woman. "Do you think it is harmful?"

"It does not seem to harm the Gyjak," said the man, "and I think there may be people who sometimes go through here."

"Have you seen any trace of them?" asked Helene. "The people, that is."

"No, I do not think this is a regular passageway for people. I do not catch any scent of them," he added, "but that does not mean they are not around somewhere."

They were passing another open doorway and Ki-Gor moved to the entrance and held the torch where the light would let them see into the dark room. He had been doing this for a moment at each doorway they passed. This time he had a quick intake of breath and backed up a step.

"What is it?" whispered Helene.

"It looked like a man!" replied her mate in a voice so low she could barely hear it.

Holding his assegai ready, Ki-Gor silently entered the room. It was a small cubicle and contained only four elegantly dressed individuals. However, they appeared almost lifelike.

"Why do these four look so realistic while all the others have been very dried out?" Helene asked as they cautiously moved about the small room.

"There is more of the gas coming up through the floor," replied Ki-Gor. "Perhaps that has something to do with... uh," he said, searching for the word.

"Preserving," said Helene.

"Yes, preserving the bodies," Ki-Gor nodded.

They spent only a couple of moments in the room before moving on in the cavern. Now, as they passed open doorways, they would see preserved remains that were near lifelike in appearance. The smoky looking gas coming up through the cracks in the floor seemed to become heavier as they advanced.

"The gas is getting thicker," said Helene, "and the bodies look more and more like they were just interred here. It must be the gas that keeps them in their current state."

"That looks like the end of the cavern just ahead of us," said Ki-Gor, "unless it is going to make another turn."

They came to a dead end. The tunnel just stopped. A wall of rock blocked their passage.

"What do we do? Go back?" asked Helene. "We have found the Smoking Caverns, but we have not found or seen any sign of Jerry and Ray."

"Perhaps there is a hidden door here somewhere," said Ki-Gor, handing Helene his torch. "Our light is not too good. It may be that we are just not seeing it."

He began to run his fingers along the stone wall, feeling for something that would indicate a doorway. Helene, still holding the torch, placed the extra ones she was carrying against a side wall. Then, with her free hand, she began helping the man feel along the wall for any indication there might be a way through.

They found nothing at the end of the tunnel. In exasperation, Helene leaned against the side wall where she had placed the unlit torches. As she did so, the wall beside Ki-Gor began to silently open.

"It is a perfectly balanced door!" the woman exclaimed. She moved away from the wall that she had leaned against, and the door stopped moving.

Ki-Gor reached out and exerted pressure. The door began moving again and as it opened, daylight flooded in from outside.

"...these four look so realistic..."

The man experimented with the door and it moved easily at his touch. It would go either direction, dictated by his hand pressure. They extinguished the torch, which was about half used up, and placed it with the unused ones inside the tunnel. They stepped outside into the daylight.

"Oh, this feels good!" exclaimed Helene.

They closed the balanced door. Then Ki-Gor tried to reopen it and the door would not budge. He exerted more pressure and still nothing.

"Perhaps I need to lean against a wall," laughed Helene.

They began looking and soon found what appeared to be a smoother area than the rest of the rock surface. The girl leaned against it and her mate pushed against the door. It opened easily.

"Okay, now we know how to get in and how to get out," Helene said.

"I think," said Ki-Gor, "the place where we entered the cavern was an air vent. It was fixed up so you could go in or out, if need be, but it was really to allow movement of air. It also gives the small Gyjak a way in and out."

"But there was no way for the flying lizards to get in or out on this end," said Helene.

"I have a feeling there are other places to get in and out. More air vents. I still believe the woman, Meca Huko, is involved with these caverns in some way," mused Ki-Gor. "I think there are other air vents and other secret doors. We just didn't happen to notice them. And I don't think that woman entered where we did. I could scent a Gyjak, but she also had a leopard with her. She was small enough to get through that hole, just as you were," he added, "but I don't think she did. I couldn't sense her or the leopard. If they came through the caverns, they had a different entrance."

"Those air vents," said the woman, "would have been necessary long ago when the Smoking Caverns were really smoking. There isn't enough of that smoke-gas coming up now to make any difference."

They were standing outside the cavern door in a depression that appeared to be man-made. The door itself was imbedded in solid rock, or so it appeared. On each side of the depression were huge boulders that abutted against the rock on each side of the door. Checking around the depression, they found where it had been fixed up to drain away rain water.

Ki-Gor and Helene moved to the outer edge of the depression and looked out over a long and wide valley with a large river winding through the middle of it. Off to the left there appeared to be a large swampy area. To the right, some distance away, they could see a dense jungle.

A trail led off to the right and seemed to stay near the slope of the ridge where they were standing.

"Wow!" said Helene, glancing upward, "that sun is much redder than what I am used to! It must be something in the atmosphere."

At that moment there came a long deep bellowing sound from some distance away. It had no sooner died away than an answering sound, similar in tone, came from another direction.

"What made those sounds?" Helene asked, looking at Ki-Gor.

The strange expression on Ki-Gor's face told Helene what she wanted to know. Her mate did not know what kind of animal had made those sounds either.

"We are here to locate the two boys, Jerry and Ray," she said. "Which way do you think we should go?"

"This is all strange to me," Ki-Gor said. "I have been on the other side of the mountains and this is not what I saw! This does not have the right feel to it."

"It is jungle, Ki-Gor," said Helene. "We are probably in a different place than where you were when you crossed the mountains."

"The sun is too red!" the man persisted. "We are in the wrong place! We should go back and try again. We will not find the boys here."

"The sun is red because of dust in the atmosphere," said Helene. "Now, which way do you think we should go to find the boys?"

"Follow the trail," the Jungle Lord said in disgust.

Helene led at a trot and they started down the trail that led by the front of the Smoking Caverns. They were gradually going downhill and the woman thought they were probably moving toward the river. She voiced her thoughts to Ki-Gor and he nodded.

"People live near water," he said.

"Then maybe we can find someone who can tell us where to go to find out about the boys we are hoping to locate!"

They had covered perhaps a quarter of a mile and were out of sight of the ridge where the Smoking Caverns were located. Helene felt good and was enjoying the run. Her first indication that anything was wrong was when she heard something that sounded like canvas flapping in the wind. She and Ki-Gor both turned to look behind them at the same time.

Helene gasped in shock. Diving toward them from above was some type of giant bird with a huge beak that was open as he reached for Ki-Gor, the nearest victim.

The jungle man was quick and he jammed the blade of his assegai through the open jaws of the flying beast. The point came out of the back of the creature's head. The thing was now on the ground but still flopping and trying to get hold of Ki-Gor with his jaws, even though it was dying. The man released his hold on the weapon and, drawing his long bladed knife, leaped astride the beast's back and began slashing at the vulnerable neck.

"No! Helene, no!" he shouted when he saw the woman drawing the pistol from the back of her belt. "Do not shoot!"

Blood was gushing from the slashed neck and the flying creature was now flopping on the ground as death claimed it.

Ki-Gor leaped away from the monster and hurried to Helene's side. Instinctively, he placed his arm around her shoulders.

"Why didn't you want me to shoot it?" she said in a raspy voice. "It could have injured you very badly!"

"I wanted you to save your bullets," said Ki-Gor softly. "I have a feeling we may need them and this thing was already dead. It just took a while for it to get there!"

"Yes, you're right," the woman said. "The only shells we have are the ones in the gun. I checked and it holds eight rounds. By the way, what is that thing?"

"I don't know," the man replied. "A leather bird? A huge flying bat? This is different than anything I have seen. The coloring is strange, more like a lizard or a snake. Perhaps those are scales on his skin." Ki-Gor was shaking his head in disbelief.

They waited until the spasmodic movements of the creature ceased, then the jungle man removed his metal assegai from the monster. With the weapon, he shoved the carcass off the trail.

"That looked like a prehistoric beast to me," said Helene as they moved down the trail.

"What is pre...?" asked Ki-Gor.

"Prehistoric," replied the woman, "is that time before history. Before mankind. In the time of the dinosaurs and when other strange creatures roamed the earth."

Ki-Gor nodded in understanding.

"I believe this thing we just killed should have been extinct a long time ago," she said. "It should not have still been around here, or anywhere else."

Ki-Gor nodded. He knew what 'extinct' meant by the way Helene used it in the sentence.

"I suppose," she continued, "there could be pockets, in wild out of the way places, where something like this creature still survived. Someplace where civilized man has not yet been."

They were not trotting, but walking at a rather fast clip and keeping a much closer watch on their surroundings than they had before their conflict with the creature.

Eventually they came to a river, but it was not the big body of water they had seen when they were up on the ridge. It was a tributary and here the trail turned and followed the running water upstream. The jungle became thicker and darker. Ki-Gor seemed deeply concerned.

"I do not like this, Helene," he said. "There is something wrong here."

"Yes, I agree," his mate replied. "We need to find the boys and get out of here."

"We do not know for sure, this is where they are," he replied.

"But where else could they be?"

"They may be in an unknown village on the other side," the man suggested.

"Let's see where this trail leads," suggested Helene, "then decide if we should stay or go back. I'd just as soon be back on the other side by nightfall."

A deep growl came from the underbrush near the trail. Ki-Gor and Helene both stopped dead in their tracks, assegais held ready. Then came a voice that was definitely human, although guttural in sound. Ki-Gor motioned silently and they both began backing up. A few quick steps and the man caught Helene by the hand and they moved into the brush on the opposite side of the trail. They ran quickly for a few paces, then they stopped and Helene was lifted where she could grab a high branch and swing into the tree. Instantly, her mate was beside her. Without hesitation they began moving along the branches putting distance between themselves and the spot where they had entered the trees. They were high enough up that the ground was not visible below them. For a hundred yards, they hurried. Then they stopped and remained quiet.

Listening, they could here the voices of men and the growling of beasts that evidently accompanied them. They heard them move down the trail and then go into the jungle.

"The beasts are following us," whispered Ki-Gor. "If they take to the trees, we will need to move quickly."

Helene nodded and they continued to listen. They heard the frustration of the warriors when they reached the spot where the spoor of Ki-Gor and Helene had disappeared. The voices and the growling rose in tempo with the disappointment of the pursuers. Finally the sounds began to fade away and Ki-Gor breathed a sigh of relief.

"Let us stay in the trees for a while," he said. "We'll go in the opposite direction of whatever those were. Then we'll get back on the trail."

The jungle began to thin somewhat as they moved through the branches and eventually they could see the ground below them.

Ki-Gor gave a soft chuckle. "The trail is directly below us," he said. "We can go down and travel on the trail."

"Until we run onto some more of those odd creatures in this strange land," smiled Helene. "Ki-Gor," she added, "I'm thirsty. Can we find a place where there is some clean water I can drink?"

"Stay right here," the jungle man said. "I will climb to the top and see what I can see out there. We know where the river is, but I do not think that it is very clean."

Ki-Gor began to rapidly scale the tree and was soon as high as his weight would allow him to go. He heard a noise and looked down to see Helene right below him.

"I try to keep you safe," he grumbled, "and what do you do?"

"I want to be with you," the woman smiled. "I want to see what you see and I want to know what you are looking for to determine where to find water."

The man chuckled and nodded. That would be Helene, alright.

"Over there," said Ki-Gor, "you see the cliffs. They are part of the ridge where we came out of the caverns. But some distance away. Do you see where the sun is shining on those gray rocks? That may be a reflection of water. If so, it should be clean enough to drink. We shall go see."

It did not take them long to get to the ground and walk the short distance to the slabs of rock that were part of the ridge. There were several places where water oozed out and trickled downward. Ki-Gor soon had a small place scooped out to catch the water. Gradually it filled up and Helene was able to slack her thirst. Then Ki-Gor drank. It took them several minutes as they would drink and then wait for the water to fill up again. Finally they were ready to go.

"Back to the trail?" asked Helene. Ki-Gor did not answer and the young woman turned to see what had his attention. He was standing, looking at the edge of the jungle about forty feet away.

When Helene looked to see what had his attention in the shadows, she saw the forms of six warriors standing there.

"Oh!" she exclaimed, startled.

"Jambo! We come in peace, my friends," said Ki-Gor in Swahili, a language understood by both he and Helene.

"Welcome," came a male voice and a fellow stepped out of the shadows.

Again, Helene did a double take as she thought she was looking at Katonga. Then she realized she was not, but there was much about this man that resembled the guide with the Jacobson safari.

The remaining five figures moved forward as well and Helene saw that there were two men and four women in the group. They were all armed the same as well as dressed very much alike. In fact, the women seemed to be dressed identical to Meca Huko as they had seen her the night previously. The men also wore the many bone and claw necklaces that covered the bare chests of both male and female.

"Do you speak English?" asked Helene.

In Swahili, Ki-Gor repeated the question about speaking English.

"No," was the reply. "We speak our tribal language and Swahili. That is all. You would come with us now."

"Where do we go?"

"We go to our village," the man replied. "We give you food and clean water." Then he grinned as though it were some kind of joke.

"We are strangers to your land," Ki-Gor said, as they fell in step with the natives. "What is this place called?"

They had only walked a few steps before Ki-Gor put the question to them, but it brought them to an immediate stop. The two leading, a man and a woman, turned to face the two white people. Their faces expressed surprise and there was a long moment of silence.

Finally the man spoke. "We are the Artobas and we live here in a land known as Tobonglan. Our country stretches two days walk in that direction," and he pointed ahead of them. "And two days walk in that direction," he added, pointing in the opposite direction. Again, there was hesitation and Ki-Gor spoke.

"I am Ki-Gor," he said. "I am from the other side of the mountains. This woman is my mate, Helene."

"I am Motribo," the man said in reply. "I have been to the other side of the mountains and it is a land full of the large beasts! I can see why you have come to Tobonglan. It is much nicer here and you are not so likely to become some creature's food!"

"We came into your country," said Ki-Gor, "looking for two lost boys. When we find them, we shall return with them to our land. Have you seen such boys?"

Motribo was about to answer when one of the female warriors at the rear of the group gave a light hissing sound and everyone became quiet. Then could be heard what sounded like muffled growling.

"Come!" Motribo commanded in a stage whisper. He turned and ran and the group, including Ki-Gor and Helene, followed. They went a very short distance, but it was an open grassy area that the man had led them to. Here they prepared to face whatever was coming.

"What?" asked Ki-Gor, who was standing beside Motribo, his assegai held ready.

Coming out of the jungle were three figures riding on what appeared to be large dogs, only they were quite wide across the shoulders, much more so than a normal domesticated dog.

The riders where short, very dark and carried wicked looking curved swords. The beast-men were covered with black hair close to four inches in length and over the entire body, excluding faces, palms of the hands and soles of the feet. The eyes were very dark and close set. As they advanced, they were waving their swords and making threatening noises. The dog-like mounts were also barking and growling. The squat riders were opening and closing their mouths, bellowing and displaying long fangs in the upper jaws, as they approached.

When they realized they were facing eight armed warriors ready to do battle, they brought their mounts to a stop and spoke among themselves.

"Why did they stop?" Ki-Gor asked of Motribo.

"I think they are trying to decide if the eight of us can create a significant loss for them if they want to continue the fight," the man replied. "Knowing them, they will have convinced themselves to continue very shortly now."

"Thrust with your spears!" shouted Motribo as the riders started toward them again. "Don't throw them! Watch their mounts as they will be as bad as the beast-men!"

The leader was half a length in front of his two companions as they approached.

"You get the rider," said Motribo to Ki-Gor, who was right beside him, "and I'll take down the mount. Watch for the jaws of either one of them!"

Working in tandem, Ki-Gor buried his assegai in the creature's chest while evading the snapping of his mount. Motribo stepped to the opposite side and rammed his spear through the rib cage of the dog-like mount. Both the rider and his mount went down, dead and dying as they hit the turf.

Ki-Gor turned immediately to see how Helene was doing. His mate had thrust her spear through the lower neck of the beast-man who was now spewing blood from his mouth. Another woman had shoved her spear into the cavernous maw of the beast-dog and he was shaking his massive head with tremendous force. The woman hung onto her weapon and the creature was lifting and swinging her to and fro as he tried to disengage himself from the deep-seated barb. He quickly went to his knees and then his eyes glazed as he dropped his head, dying. Another woman had also planted her spear in the creature's side while he was still struggling.

The remaining man and two women had taken on the third beast-man and his mount. One of the women had skewered the fellow on her spear, forcing him from his seat on the beast-dog. Her two companions caught the snarling creature from each side and quickly dispatched him.

The battle was over in an exceedingly short time. Miraculously, none of Motribo's group, including Ki-Gor and Helene, had suffered any wounds, not even a scratch. The two men went around to the downed beast-men and slit their throats to make sure they were dead.

"We were very fortunate," said Motribo. "I do not believe I have ever been in a fight with the beast-men where no one was injured!"

"We did have them outnumbered eight to three," said Helene with a smile.

"It was more like eight to six," said Motribo, "because their mounts are trained to kill and they are good at it. There have been times when all the beast-men and all the warriors have been slaughtered but some of the beast-dogs have survived! They just kept fighting until there was no one left to fight! We were fortunate!"

"I believe," said Helene, looking at the leader of the Artobas, "that your choice of where to do battle was a major reason for our success!"

Motribo nodded and smiled. "Yes," he agreed, "giving ourselves room to spread out and take them on unhindered, was an advantage."

"Those things had to be what was following us," said Ki-Gor to Helene. "I'm glad we did not try to fight them by ourselves!"

"Motribo," said Ki-Gor, as they walked along, "just before the beast-men came, we had asked you about the two boys. Do you know of them?"

"Were they white boys such as you and your woman?"

"Yes," replied Ki-Gor. "Their father is very worried about them." Then he wondered just how much Gabe Jacobson really cared about the welfare of the two boys.

"The boys are not your sons?"

"No," replied Ki-Gor, "we are just trying to find them for their father."

"One of the men last night," replied Motribo, thoughtfully, "said something about two strangers being brought to be treated for poison. Then they were taken to our leaders in Vashkin. I do not know that they were young boys, though. I was thinking they were grown men, but perhaps..." and the man hesitated. Then he asked, "Did they, by any chance, have the odd hair coloring of you and your mate? Is that your real color or have you done something to it? At first, I thought you were just very old, Ki-Gor, but you do not fight like an old man."

"I believe they had dark hair like their father," said Ki-Gor. "Neither my mate, nor I have actually seen them. We are just trying to help find them. We were given to believe that they had been bitten by something, but we are not sure about that."

"Then perhaps the two you seek were taken to Vaskin. We will be in our village before long and I will ask and see if anyone knows anything about two boys," said Motribo.

"Do you know a man named Katonga?" asked Helene.

There was silence for a few moments and the woman thought she was not going to get a reply to her question. Then Motribo rubbed his head. "Yes, I know Katonga," he said. "He belongs to our tribe, the Artobas. But he is not around much. I have not seen him in a long time." Helene nodded without reply.

They were silent from that time onward as they made the trek to the village of the Artobas. When they arrived, Helene and Ki-Gor were assigned a straw grass thatched hut and told that food would be brought to them. Inside there were many furs and blankets that gave the place a pleasant appearance. There was a place in the center of the hut where a fire could be ignited.

"I believe," said Ki-Gor, "that the nights may be colder than what we are used to on the other side of the mountains."

Helene nodded. "I think there is more going on here than we are aware of, especially in their knowledge of the two boys, Jerry and Ray."

"Yes," agreed Ki-Gor, "and I think we need to be careful what we say in English."

"But," said Helene with a frown on her face, "they said they did not speak English. So do you think they were being dishonest?"

"Perhaps," said Ki-Gor softly. "Perhaps not. They said they spoke Swahili and their own tribal language. They said they did not speak English. They didn't actually say they couldn't, just that they didn't. Twice I have felt like they knew something that they would have to know English to know about us."

"What was that?" asked Helene.

"When they first arrived," said Ki-Gor, "Motribo made a comment about you drinking clean water. He could have only known that if he had been listening to us before we knew he was there. And we were speaking only English."

"Okay," smiled Helene, "I see what you mean. It's okay to speak English, just don't say anything important! Right?"

Ki-Gor chuckled and nodded.

"You could have used your pistol on those beast-men," said Ki-Gor, changing the topic, "but I'm glad you didn't. We may need that as a surprise later."

"This village seems to be very clean," said Helene, "which surprises me. And I have seen no children running around playing and making noise. It seems there aren't any, which may be why the village seems to be clean."

"This hut is certainly clean," replied the man.

"I wonder," said the woman, "are we guests, prisoners or are we just visitors? What do you think?"

"I don't know," Ki-Gor replied. "I think when we first started out, we may have actually been prisoners. But it would be easier to let us keep our weapons and just walk along with them in friendship until we reached the village. But then the beast-men showed up and we were a definite help in taking care of them. Then I think we became visitors."

"Let's go out and walk around a little bit," said Helene. "I am tired but I want to see where we are. Just get a feel for the place."

Ki-Gor and Helene had moved about the village for several minutes without anyone actually paying any attention to them. They did not see any children and they did not see any old people, which, in both cases, seemed out of the ordinary.

The village was surrounded by a stockade made of tall wooden poles. The settlement, which numbered some twenty huts, sat back a short distance from the trail which ran within fifty yards of one gate. There was a second gate located at the rear of the village.

"I can see having two gates," said Ki-Gor. "You wouldn't want to be trapped in your own village without an avenue of escape. And I see both of them are open, so I am wondering what lies outside the back gate. Let's walk that way and see if we can find out."

They had almost reached the gate when a young girl came running up. She looked young, but then everyone they had seen could fit that category. This girl, however, was just slightly shorter than the other village females. And she was dressed exactly like everyone else in the village, including the many necklaces that covered her bare chest.

"...are we guests, prisoners or...just visitors?"

"Please excuse me for bothering you," she said, panting slightly and smiling, "but I would like to ask you some questions, if you do not mind. Would that be permissible?"

"Of course," said Helene, smiling in return. "What would you like to know?"

"It is about your hair," she said softly, wistfulness in her voice. "Is it the right color or do you change the color somehow? Yours," she said, looking at Ki-Gor, "is so white! It is beautiful! I have never seen anything like it! And yours," she said, turning back to Helene, "it has so much red to the color! Is it naturally red like that? It, too, is very beautiful!"

"Ki-Gor's hair and my hair are the right colors for us," smiled Helene. "We come from a different race of people. My hair is very much the right color, but I think Ki-Gor's hair would be more of a yellow color, or blond, but it is bleached from being in the sun so much! And you have noticed that our eyes are blue, have you not? That is their regular color, too. Now in Ki-Gor's case, his eyes sometimes seem to become a cloudy gray but I think that comes mostly when it is a really cloudy day. But there have been other times when I think his eyes change when he becomes agitated."

The young woman nodded and smiled at the visitors in her village. "I am the one who is to bring food to you when it becomes time to eat," and she smiled again.

"Speaking of eating," said Helene, "just when does that take place?"

"Any time now," the girl replied. "Just whenever you feel like you want to eat. Let me know and I will bring your food to you. Oh, my name is Laketna. If you do not see me, just ask someone where to find Laketna and they will tell you."

"I believe we will be ready to eat soon," said Ki-Gor. "We would like to go out the back gate and take a look around. That won't take long. Then we will be ready for some food."

"Do you mind if I go out the back gate with you?" the woman asked. "A path leads down to the river where there are several boats moored by the dock."

"Sure," said Helene, "come along. We may have questions to ask and you would be a good one to explain things to us."

As it turned out, the back side of the village opened out on the river. The village was situated on a bluff and there were steps cut in the rock leading down to the dock at river level. As there were several large canoes, or boats, moored to the docks, Ki-Gor was interested in going down and looking at them.

Laketna kept up a constant chatter with Helene as they descended. Ki-Gor listened but did not contribute much to the conversation.

When they reached the level of the boats, the jungle man realized they were much larger than had been his first impression from atop the bluff. They were constructed in such a manner as to seat two rowers side by side for five rows. That would make for ten rowers and Ki-Gor could see where the light vessel could make very good speed over the water. There were four such boats moored at the dock and they all seemed to be the same size.

"With ten rowers per boat," said Ki-Gor, "that would take forty men to launch all four of the boats at the same time. But I only counted about twenty houses in your village. It seems you could only use about two boats at a time. Maybe three if you didn't have as many rowers in each one."

"Ki-Gor," smiled Laketna, "you are forgetting that in our village, the men and women all share all work loads the same. We all do the same things. I know that not every group does that, but we do." Then she laughed again.

"One exception," she said, looking at the big jungle man, "and that is bearing children, which does not happen very often."

Ki-Gor nodded and his attention went back to the boats. "Your village, with both men and women warriors, could fill all four boats," and he nodded as though agreeing with himself.

"Laketna, I noticed there do not seem to be any children in your village," said Helene, coming back to the idea of bearing young. "Nor have I seen any elderly people?"

Laketna was silent for a moment, then she grinned at Helene. "When we get back to your lodge," she said, "and I have brought you food, we will talk. There is much about the Artobas that is different from the tribes that live farther away. We will talk more," she said.

As Ki-Gor looked over the canoes, he was impressed. The main hull seemed to be carved from one tree trunk with the seats being attached later. The prow of the boat had a tall piece in a fixed upright position and he wondered if it was used to fly a pennant or flag of some sort. The rear of the craft had a similar piece, but it was more of a flat board that arched over and went into the water. There appeared to be a grip where someone standing in the rear of the boat could hang on and Ki-Gor wondered if it might have something to do with steering the craft. The more he looked at the piece, the more sure he was that it operated like a rudder.

"How often do your warriors take these boats out on the water?" he asked.

"Almost daily," the woman replied. "We do much fishing as the river is a good source of food. We have a place down there," she added, pointing, "where all the cleaning takes place. That keeps the fish odor out of our village."

"I am impressed with your village," said Helene. "I don't know that I have seen a village or settlement anywhere, Africa or North America, that is as clean. It is really nice." Then she saw the look of confusion of Laketna's face.

"Oh," she said, in a quick explanation, "those are places far away from here."

The woman smiled and nodded as the three turned to retrace their steps back to the village on the bluff.

"You are ready for your evening meal?" asked Laketna, when the reached the back gate.

Both Ki-Gor and Helene nodded. It had been a full day and they were hungry.

"You go to your lodge," said Laketna and I shall return shortly with your meal.

"I still have difficulty getting used to the idea there are no children or elderly people here," said Helene to Ki-Gor as the Artobas woman disappeared.

Ki-Gor and Helene had not been in the hut assigned to them very long before Laketna appeared with a pole across her shoulders. From each end hung two woven nets wrapped around food stuffs and eating utensils.

The woman placed her load gently on the floor and, from behind a skin at one side of the room, produced a low table. This she sat near the center of the room, close to the circle of stones surrounding the fire pit.

Both Ki-Gor and Helene were amazed at the amount of food she produced from her supplies. There was soup, vegetables, fruit and strips of roasted meat. She sat out three places and joined her new friends in their meal.

There were several items of food that neither Ki-Gor nor Helene was familiar with and they asked the woman about them. Laketna was in a talkative mood and was happy to explain as much as she could about their questions.

"Laketna," said Helene, when they were almost finished with the repast, "you were going to explain why there are no children or elderly members of your tribe in this village."

"Oh, yes," the woman replied with a smile. "It has been this way for a long time. Long before I was born. You see, children are rarely born to the

Artobas. Also, our life span is considerably longer than other tribes."

"In that case," commented Helene, "I would think we would see more elderly people in your village."

"You do," replied Leketna, "you just don't realize how old they are. You see, probably for the same reason we do not reproduce very often, we do not show aging. We will live for perhaps a hundred fifty years or more. We will appear to remain about the same age all during that time. However, for a short time before we pass on, we will age tremendously. And then we will be gone. The aging thing all happens between ten and fifteen days. Once you begin to age, you have just a short amount of time before your body shuts down."

"Oh!" exclaimed Helene. "That is different!"

There was a brief moment of silence and then Helene asked the question. "Just how old are you, Laketna? You appear to us to be in your early twenties. You are a very beautiful young woman."

"Thank you," said Laketna, obviously pleased with the compliment. "I am about sixty years old now. Most of my life is still ahead of me. I would still be able to reproduce for another forty years, but after that, not likely."

"If your people do not reproduce very often," asked Helene, "how do you keep your numbers up? It seems like you would soon all be deceased."

"When you don't die your numbers stay very much the same, only when there is an accident and someone gets killed. Or in battle, such as you were in with the beast-men before you arrived in our village. Over time, it has lessened our numbers."

"Do you take children from other tribes?" asked Ki-Gor, thinking of Jerry and Ray.

"Sometimes," Leketna replied, "but that is usually a situation where the child has no place to go. Then we take him to Vaskin."

"Vashkin?" questioned Helene.

"Oh, that is where our children are raised and educated. When they reach twelve years of age, they are taught to be warriors and generally come back to the original city of their birth when they reach about fifteen or sixteen years of age."

"They are taken away from their mothers?" asked Helene.

"Not exactly," Laketna replied. "The mother goes with them when they are very young. When they reach about a year and a half in age, the mother returns to her village."

"You mean they do not see their child again until it has reached fifteen or sixteen years of age?" asked Helene.

"Oh, the mother can go visit her child quite often. But it is important that the child not get to depending strictly on just its own mother, which would happen if she would be allowed to stay. She can visit as often as once every ten days. Then she has to be gone for nine days before she can visit again," explained the woman.

"What about the husband?" asked Ki-Gor. "Does he not get to see his son?"

Laketna looked a little confused. "I do not understand," she finally said.

"Your mate," explained Helene. "The warrior who fathered your child, does he not get to see his children as does the mother?"

"Oh," said the woman, smiling. "Now I understand. Long, long ago, so far back in time we do not know just how long anymore, our people would mate with each other. That is, a man and a woman would choose to live together. Then as time changed and we began to live longer lives, and we did not reproduce very often, the need for living together vanished. Now we just hope that in a hundred years time our village might produce twenty births. Many females never give birth. Others may give birth to two or three children. We know," said Laketna, with tears in her eyes, "that the time is coming when the Artobas will exist no more! It is sad."

"Yes," agreed Helene.

"I believe," said Ki-Gor softly, "that you know more about us than you might be inclined to let us know. What can you tell us about the two boys we are hoping to find?"

Ki-Gor and Helene were sitting side-by-side on the opposite side of the fire pit facing the door. They were not touching each other as they were about a foot apart. Leketna was on the opposite side of the pit, facing them with her back to the open doorway.

Silently she rose to her feet, moved to the opposite side of the eating arrangement and squeezed in between Ki-Gor and Helene.

"I must be careful what I say," she whispered. "I must face the door so I can see if someone comes. It must appear that I am very friendly with you and your mate," she said to Helene.

Ki-Gor's face remained stoic but Helene frowned slightly.

"I am not to tell you this," the woman began in a whisper. "Sometimes we have warriors that go through the Smoking Cavern and into the world on the other side. We have had warriors cross over the mountains, but it seems that there are two different worlds. If you cross the mountains, you come to a land that is populated with huge beasts. If you go through the cavern, you come to a place, while it also has beasts, they are not so large.

And they also have people there. Now, that is the place from which you have come. It is obvious."

The woman was silent as Ki-Gor and Helene seemed to be thinking about what she had said.

"You have asked about two young boys," the Artobas woman continued. "Sometimes we have someone who goes to the other side of the mountains, mostly through the Smoking Cavern, and will return with someone from the other side. This person often becomes member of a group on this side. Two boys were brought back a day ago. It seems they were lost and just wandering on the other side. We do not steal or kidnap anyone. We take them when it appears they have no other place to go."

"Were the two boys pale skinned," asked Helene, "such as Ki-Gor and me?"

Laketna nodded. "Their skin was even lighter," she added. "They were much like the two of you, but they had dark hair."

"Where are these boys now?" asked Helene. "We would like to take them back to their father. He is worried about them."

"They were taken to Vaskin," the woman whispered.

"Where is Vaskin?" asked Ki-Gor. "How do we get there?"

"Isn't that the place where you send your children to be raised?" asked Helene.

"Yes," nodded Laketna to Helene. Then she looked up at Ki-Gor. "Vaskin is our main city. Our important leaders reside there. By now they will have already started working with the two new boys and they may be reluctant to give them up. They may be very antagonistic toward you and your mate."

"They have basically taken the two boys against their will," said Helene. "Kidnapped might be a better term for it. Surely they would be willing to let them return to their father and their homeland?"

"They are very careful before they bring anyone here," said Laketna, "but once here, they consider them part of our world and are unwilling to let them go."

"We were told," added Helene, "that the boys had been poisoned and had been taken to a village where they could be treated. But they came here instead."

"Oh," said the woman, "I did not know that. It is possible they are considered belonging to the person who saved their lives and they should remain here."

"That sounds like they are considered slaves," said the red headed woman. "Do you have slavery here?"

"There is an occasional slave," said Laketna, "but generally there are not many slaves. Maybe one per village."

"Do you have one in this village?"

"No," the woman smiled. "Now, I have told you much that I should not have shared with you. Tomorrow, Motribo, who is our leader, plans to take you to Vaskin. He will let you determine what you are going to do once you get there and find out what the situation is. I have already told you more than you were supposed to know. I would ask that you try not to get me in trouble with our village leaders. Just don't say anything."

"Where is Vaskin and how do we get there?" asked Ki-Gor.

"It is upriver, in the direction from which you came today. It is a long journey, but Motribo will take you in one of our canoes," Laketna said softly.

"There will have to be a number of paddlers, won't there?" asked Helene.

"Yes," woman nodded. "There will be ten paddlers, Motribo and the two of you. I do not know who will be doing the paddling, but I may be one of them. I hope so."

"Is this a long journey?"

"We go quite fast when we have all the paddlers, which we will have for this trip," the woman replied. "But we are going against the current. I think Motribo will stay close to the shore as the current will not be so strong. In the middle of the river it is very strong but hardly ever does anyone bother you out there. Along the edge, sometimes we cross paths with the Charpos or the Genlore. They like to fight and we try to avoid them."

"It could be a dangerous trip, couldn't it?" asked Helene.

Laketna nodded.

They were silent for a moment and then Helene stood up. "If we are going to have a long hard trip tomorrow," she said, "I would like to get a good night's sleep."

She began helping the Artobas woman gather up the items from their meal and they soon had everything packed in the netting.

"I will bring you morning food," said Laketna, "about daylight. Motribo will want to get on the river shortly after that."

Helene nodded and she and Ki-Gor waved as the woman shouldered her load and left with a quick smile.

The following morning Ki-Gor and Helene were on the dock with Motribo and his paddlers, of which Laketna was one. There was a fog hanging over the water and it was almost chilly as they loaded the boat. The rowers took their positions first, then Helene was given a place in the front of the canoe. Ki-Gor was positioned in the rear of the craft and Motribo explained that balance was important to get the best speed.

"Is there any kind of danger on the river?" asked Ki-Gor, as he settled down.

"What do you mean?" asked the Artobas leader, a confused expression on his face.

"Large river creatures," said the blond giant. "Perhaps other tribes or groups that do not want you on their portion of the river. I just wondered what to be prepared for," the man explained.

"Oh," said Motribo, smiling, "I thought perhaps you were asking about water falls or rapids, that sort of thing."

"I just thought there might be conflict with enemy warriors," Ki-Gor said.

"There could be," Motribo nodded. "If such were to occur, it would come from the other side of the river. Along those shores, the Charpos and the Genlore claim the land and the river."

Ki-Gor nodded quietly and placed his assegai on the bottom of the boat. It would be difficult to have it ready for quick use, but there was no other place to carry it. Helene, in the prow of the boat, saw how her mate placed his weapon and she did the same.

The large canoe began to move and the paddlers quickly fell into a synchronized effort. They moved away from the shore only far enough to have clear water for the rowers, as close to the shore were many kinds of plant growth including moss and cattails among the stagnant water. The fellow just behind Ki-Gor guiding the craft by the rudder explained to the jungle man that the water along the shore was slow moving and therefore easier to travel when going against the current.

Time passed rather quickly for Ki-Gor and Helene as there was always something to view as the canoe skimmed along. At midmorning, Motribo slowed his crew and they worked their way to shore as it was time for the workers to take a break.

"I think we are at least even with, if not past, the point where we came out of those caverns," said Ki-Gor to Helene, referring to the mountains behind them as they stood looking across the river.

The woman nodded in agreement and then said, "This river certainly is wide, Ki-Gor. I'm glad we are not out in the middle somewhere. It seems to be flowing really fast out there."

"I don't think our crew could gain much paddling against that current. It is very strong. Now if we were going the other direction, down river, we would just be flying along!"

Laketna moved over and stood beside them as they gazed across the moving water of the river.

"This is really a large river," commented the jungle man. "It winds around enough that it creates many spots where the water is slow and sluggish. I would think there would be many different kinds of creatures living there."

"There are," agreed Laketna. "We just haven't come across any yet. But we may. Usually it does not take much to discourage them. And for the really big ones, we are moving too fast for them to take much interest in us."

"What about other groups of warriors?" asked Ki-Gor. "Certainly not everyone is your friend in this area."

"There are two groups on the other side of the river," the woman said. "They are the Charpos, who are directly across from where we are now. Then another hour and half up the river we will be passing by the territory claimed by the Genlore. They are often in disagreement with each other. They seldom come to this side of the river, so we do not usually have any problem with them as we go upriver. Now, coming downstream when we are farther out from the banks to take advantage of the quick flowing current, they sometimes come out to harass us."

"When will we reach Vaskin?" asked Helene.

"Early afternoon," Laketna replied.

"And what are the plans when we reach there?"

"You will meet with our Queen and ask for the return of your two boys, if they happen to be in Vaskin," the woman replied. "It is possible they are not the ones you are searching for. Or they may have been taken somewhere else."

Motribo gave a call and they began loading into the canoe. Soon they were moving again over the sluggish water near the shoreline.

They had been moving for close to half an hour when Motribo gave a warning call. Ahead of them was a canoe coming in their direction.

"Charpos!" came the identification when they were still some distance away. "Ki-Gor! Helene!" came Motribo's clear voice. "Crouch down. Try to be inconspicuous."

"Is the water safe?" Ki-Gor asked the man at the rudder.

The fellow just shrugged. With that, the jungle man leaned over the edge of the boat and slipped into the water. He surfaced and hung onto the edge of the canoe as it moved slowly forward.

Ahead, Helene looked back and saw what her mate and done. Immediately, she began moving to the offside of the boat with the intent of slipping into the water with him.

"No!" came Ki-Gor's command.

She looked back at her husband and saw him signal for her to stay seated in the canoe.

"I think they want to fight," came Motribo's voice. "And they do have us outnumbered! Do not throw your spears. Keep them in your hands for thrusting!"

The warriors in the approaching boat numbered some two dozen men. They were armed with swords and carried shields for deflecting thrusts by an enemy. Their canoe was a good deal larger than the one occupied by the Artobas.

"Keep thrusting with your spears," said Motribo. "We must keep their boat at a distance so they cannot reach us easily with their swords."

"Motribo!" came a call from the approaching Charpos boat. "What have you brought us today?"

"I see a pale woman! Would she be a gift for the Charpos?" and laughter came from the approaching boat.

At this point, Ki-Gor slipped under the murky water and disappeared from sight. Only the fellow by the rudder saw him duck under the water, but he had no time to think about what might be the purpose.

The jungle man moved strongly toward the enemy craft, staying deep enough to be unnoticed as he neared the canoe. He passed under the boat and came up on the back side. He gently broke the surface of the water and took a deep breath. The Charpos were intent on the Artobas and were totally unaware of the pale skinned man in the water.

The Charpos had begun chanting as they approached the smaller vessel. Their noise covered any sound Ki-Gor may have made as he submerged and stroked toward the head of the canoe where the leader was standing. When he surfaced he was right beside the large canoe. He grabbed the edge and swung himself upward. With two hands, he shoved the leader overboard and then, grasping the decorative figurehead that protruded upward from the bow, he swung outward. This immediately tipped the canoe and the Charpos warriors tumbled into the water.

Ki-Gor held onto the figurehead and rode it into the water, turning the boat completely over. As he was coming into the water, the enemy leader surfaced, still holding his sword in one hand. The jungle man turned and kicked at the fellow just before he hit the water again. He got a solid connection with his heel on the fellow's head. Stunned, the fellow tried to get his sword into play, but Ki-Gor had gone under water.

The Jungle Lord now pulled his knife and came again at the Charpos

...he shoved the leader overboard...

leader. The sword stroke was ineffective and then Ki-Gor closed, his long blade driving deep and hard into the chest of the fellow. There was a gasping gurgle and the area around them turned a muddy red.

Ki-Gor ripped the sword from the hand of the dying man and turned back toward the overturned boat. Without hesitation, he rammed the long blade through the bottom of the vessel. He twisted the blade and turned it sharply, causing the hole to widen immensely. He ripped the blade out and moved down the boat where he repeated his destruction of the boat.

When Ki-Gor was satisfied with his handiwork on the enemy vessel, he turned to see the Charpos trying to get away from the thrusting spears of the laughing Artobas. There were several dead bodies in the water and the survivors were trying to get out of reach of the deadly thrusts of those spears.

Ki-Gor was sure the blood in the water would attract creatures that he did not want to face. He stroked immediately for the Artobas canoe. In his right hand he still held the sword he had taken from the Charpos leader as he felt that he might need it before he could get to safety.

The prow of the boat was the closest and he made for that immediately. He could hear Helene calling to him as he approached and thought she was trying to warn him of something. Then a submerged beast brushed against him. Instinctively, he thrust out with the long sword. He felt it bite into something. Then he was by the boat and arms were helping pull him to safety.

Then he was lying in the boat, panting, and Helene was kneeling beside him. He realized he was bleeding from either cuts or scratches, perhaps both, from his chest. He sat up and looked down at his feet but both legs seemed fine.

The boat was moving as all the rowers were back in position except where Ki-Gor was in the way. There was a turmoil of splashing water and unrecognizable sounds as the monsters of the river fed on the unfortunate warriors who did not make it to shore.

"Ki-Gor," came Motribo's exultant voice, "that had to be the bravest thing I have ever seen a man do!"

"It seemed the thing to do," replied the jungle man. "If I had time to think about it, I probably would not have done it! However, I did get a nice sword out of it!" and he held up the sword that had been placed beside him.

Helene smiled. "Have you looked at the handle yet, Ki-Gor?" she asked.

The man shook his head as he turned the sword so that he could look at the handle which had an intricately woven piece for protection of the wielder's hand. Known as a basket handle, this one had a great number of small stones set in it. And they glittered in the light as Ki-Gor held it up.

"They sparkle a lot," he observed.

"The handle is absolutely beautiful, Ki-Gor," said Helene. "I wonder if the stones have any value?"

"What I wonder," said Motribo, "is where old Whayka got it. The Charpos certainly didn't produce it themselves. He had to have taken it from someone somewhere. And that someone was very likely someone of some importance. I believe those stones are legitimate jewels, my friends!"

"Do you have something to use to stop Ki-Gor's bleeding?" asked Helene. "There are a couple of those nasty gashes that are seeping pretty good and we need to get them stopped."

"Yes," replied Motribo, "we are going to paddle for about another ten minutes, so that we will be far away from some very disgruntled Charpos! Then we will head to the shore where we can care for any wounded. And some of our rowers could use the rest after that battle back there! It didn't last long, but it was certainly intense!"

It was mid afternoon when they rounded a bend in the river and ahead of them lay the capital city of Vaskin. It was set back from the river a short distance and the structures seemed to be placed against the dark gray wall that formed the row of cliffs behind it. They appeared to be like blocks stacked on top of each other, with each level being smaller than the level below it. There were wharves along the edge of the river with dozens of various sized boats moored there. Directly behind the waterfront area and uphill was a business district and most of it was conducted outdoors. While it wasn't exactly crowded, there were numerous people conducting business and trading.

Motribo and his paddlers moored their boat and were ready to go into the city of Vaskin. The Artobas leader stopped and looked a Ki-Gor, a somewhat crooked smile on his face.

The men and women from the boat just waved at their leader and went on into the city. Only Laketna stayed with Helene, Ki-Gor and Motribo.

"That is a nice sword," the Artobas leader said, "and I have no problem with you just carrying it out in the open the way you are now, but I don't think the people on the government level will want you to carry it unsheathed. There is a leather shop up the street a short distance. Let us go there and see if we can find a sheath or scabbard for you to use in carrying your sword."

Ki-Gor gave a slight smile and nodded.

"You do give the appearance," said Helene softly, "of being ready to step into combat! That would not favor us in asking for the return of the two boys. It looks like we are ready to fight whoever has them!"

Ki-Gor smiled at his mate.

They quickly found the leather shop and the proprietor soon had a sheath of just the right length for the blade.

"Sure is a nice piece you've got there," he said. "You wouldn't consider trading or selling it, would you?"

"No," replied Ki-Gor softly. "I want to keep it."

The man nodded and Motribo handed him some coins.

"We will need to repay you in some way," said Helene as they returned to the street.

Motribo stopped and looked at the jungle couple. Then he shook his head and grinned. "What Ki-Gor did back there on the river, is worth so much more than the cost of a scabbard, that there is no comparison. He, perhaps, saved the lives of everyone on our boat! For something like that, you cannot put a price on it!"

"Oh," said Helene, "in that case, we certainly thank you!"

"We shall go directly to the top level," said Motribo, "as there is where our leaders are and that is where we can find out if the two boys you are searching for are here."

They entered one of the lower buildings and found it to be airy and spacious with many open areas. They went directly to a center wall and began climbing stair steps that went up the side. On the second level they went to a second flight of steps and went up again. After the fourth flight, they came out on a level area where they could look for long distances in either direction.

"Look at that!" exclaimed Helene. "The city stretches on for a long distance in both directions! There are a great many more people here than I had imagined!"

"What I see," said Ki-Gor, "is that many of the people are not of the same tribe as our friends. The Artobas seem to be far fewer than any of the other groups."

"I have seen some young children," whispered the woman, "but none that appeared to be Artobas."

They were approaching a doorway by which two guards were stationed.

The men were armed with both swords and spears. Motribo stopped and spoke to one of the men. The fellow gazed over the group intently and then nodded. They went through the doorway into a small room that had a number of pieces of furniture, most of which was covered by colorful hides.

Motribo crossed the room and pulled on a hanging rope. There was a faint sound in the distance.

"It will be a few minutes before anyone gets here," said Motribo. "Let us sit and wait. Climbing all those stairs was rather tiresome."

Once they were all seated, the Artobas leader spoke again. "When they come for us," he said, "do not speak unless you are spoken directly to and a response is required. You may carry your weapons but do not raise them or remove anything from its scabbard. Just don't make any sign of confrontation. There are guards you will see and there are guards you will not see."

Laketna looked a little surprised and somewhat bewildered.

"You have been here before, haven't you?" asked Helene.

"Yes," the woman nodded, "but it was a long time ago. There is much I have forgotten."

Before long there was a jingling of bells and several people, both men and women, entered the room carrying large ferns that were used as fans. They slowly moved the stalks back and forth as they walked creating a movement of air in the room.

Motribo stood and his companions followed his lead, rising to their feet. The fan bearers formed a lane directly to the visitors. Then a figure emerged from the shadows and moved down the lane to the waiting group. She smiled at them and Helene was just certain that she was indeed, this time, looking at Meco Huko.

"Motribo, it has been a long while since you have graced us with your presence," said the Queen of Tobonglan. "We welcome you! Tell us what brings you here," she said.

Helene had a strong feeling the Queen wasn't all that pleased that Motribo was actually there. She wondered if there was some kind of riff between the governing body and the Artobas people.

"I would tell you about..." but the Queen broke in and he stopped speaking quickly.

"What of these strangers?" she asked. "They do not appear to be from Tobonglan? Am I right?"

"Yes, my Queen," said Motribo. "The man is Ki-Gor and the woman is Helene. They are mates and they are from beyond the mountains."

"Ah, from the land of the giant lizards! I am surprised more of their people do not come over here where it is much nicer. Tell me about them, Motribo," the Queen commanded.

"This is their second day here," said the Artobas leader. "Yesterday, we found them near the stone cliffs not far from our village. We were taking them back to our village when we were attacked by the beast-men. Both Ki-Gor and Helene helped us defeat them without a single injury to our party. They each killed one of the beast-men."

"Commendable," murmured the Queen.

"Today, coming up the river to Vaskin," continued Motribo, "we were attacked on the water by Whayka and his Charpos. They had us outnumbered two to one. When they came in for the attack, Ki-Gor slipped out of the boat and swam underwater to their boat. When he surfaced, he was able to capsize the boat, throwing all their warriors into the water. He slew Whayka and took his sword from him. The blood in the water drew the river monsters but we got Ki-Gor into our boat before they got to him and we left immediately. Some of the Charpos made it to shore, but I am guessing perhaps half of them did not!"

The Queen turned and clapped her hands slightly. Immediately a big fellow appeared.

"You heard Motribo's narrative, did you not, Guffee?" she asked.

"Yes," the man nodded with lowered head.

"Good! Those Charpos should still be on the river bank as their boat was destroyed. Take two dozen warriors and go round them up! Move quickly now!"

The man murmured something, wheeled about and left immediately.

"You said the fellow took Whayka's sword?" asked the Queen, looking at Motribo. She still ignored both Ki-Gor and Helene.

"Yes, my Queen," replied Motribo, "he did!"

"I would see it!" she demanded.

For a moment everything was silent in the room. Then the Artobas leader turned slowly to Ki-Gor. "You may show her the sword," he said softly. "Draw it out slowly and present it to her hilt first. Make every movement very slowly."

Ki-Gor drew the sword slowly, although perhaps not as slowly as Motribo and Laketna would have liked. Both had a sharp intake of breath.

The hilt of the sword sparkled beautifully as the jungle man handed it to the Queen of Tobonglan. Her face broke into a wide smile as she received the weapon.

"It is as beautiful as the legends say!" she exclaimed. "I did not believe that old Whayka had it! I wonder how he came to possess it?"

"He had to have stolen it," said Motribo.

"But this fellow here," and the Queen glanced at Ki-Gor, "took it from Whayka in combat. That makes it legally his!"

The Queen turned and took a couple of steps in Ki-Gor's direction. "Why don't you do the right thing," she said, "and give the sword to your Queen? It would be very much appreciated!"

"You may speak, Ki-Gor," whispered Motribo, after a moment's silence.

"I do not have a Queen to give the sword to," replied Ki-Gor. "I think I will just keep it!"

The Queen's eyes narrowed and her face grew hard as she clenched her hands into fists. "To the games!" she said loudly. "That is how we will settle this!"

In a huff, she turned and left the room with her entourage scurrying to keep up with her. When the room was cleared, there remained only the four visitors surrounded by four of the palace guards.

"How many of these fellows are there just out of sight?" asked Ki-Gor.

"How many?" asked Motribo, turning to the nearest guard.

"None that I know of, Motribo," said the man.

"Then you four are the only ones in our way, if we should decide to escape, right?"

"We are to guard the Queen," grinned the man. "We aren't going to fight such a warrior as that Ki-Gor fellow you have with you!"

"I need to know a couple of things," said the Artobas leader. "First, what did the Queen mean by the 'games' and do you know anything about two young boys being brought in here a day or two ago?"

"There are two young boys in cells down by the arena," said the guard. "And by the games, I think she meant that she would put Ki-Gor into the arena against odds that would result in his death. If he dies in the arena, then whatever he owns belongs to the Queen. That is the law."

"That sounds about like our Queen," said another guard.

"When would these games take place?" asked Motribo.

"Whenever the Queen decides," was the reply.

"In other words, anytime now, right?"

All four guards nodded.

"Take us down to the cells immediately," said Motribo. "Perhaps we can find the two boys and make our escape before anyone is aware of what we are doing. You guards can get away from the area quickly, as I don't think anyone knows exactly, for sure, who was responsible for getting us down there."

Two guards led the way, then came the four prisoners, followed by the remaining two guards. They went back into the cliffs through hallways lit by glowing torches. The way went downward by ramps and occasionally by stair steps.

"These torches along the walls," said Helene, "they are not burning. What makes them give off light like they do?"

"Something in the crushed stone from which they are made," said La-ketna. "They have hundreds of them and they will glow for about a day, then they are replaced. To make them glow again, they are placed out in the direct sunlight."

Helene nodded, then she turned to Ki-Gor. "I was just certain we were looking at Meca Huko this time," she said. "Do you think it was her?"

Ki-Gor shook his head. "The scent was not hers."

At long last, they came to an area where there were cells on both sides of the hallways.

"There are several tunnels leading into the arena," said the warrior who seemed to be friends with Motribo. "I am sure the two boys are down here. We just have to find them."

"Yes," replied Motribo. "Also, is there a quick way out of here?"

"You have to go through the arena," the fellow said. "There is a wooden door directly opposite of where the Queen and her dignitaries will be seat-ed. It opens up to the outside. It is barred from the inside to keep beasts or people from getting in from the outside. Just remove the bar and open the door. You will find yourself in a cave-like area. Go through it and you will come out on a shelf that is a break in the cliff wall. It goes for some distance and then drops downward. The jungle is less than a hundred strides away."

Ki-Gor went to the end of the hallway and cautiously opened the heavy wooden door a crack. Peering out, he could see the door far to his left. Glancing to his right, he could see the lodge where the Queen and her ad-visors would sit. And he could also see people gathering in the area. They were arriving very quickly!

"I found the boys," came Motribo's voice. The two boys, Jerry and Ray, tears streaming down their faces, ran to join the group. Helena and La-ketna held out their arms to them.

"We are going to be leaving here very quickly now," said Helene. "Just make sure you stay up with us as we may be doing some fighting!"

Jerry and Ray both nodded. As yet, neither had said a word.

"The escape door is on the left," explained Ki-Gor. "People are already entering the seats, so they must be going to start this game thing soon now.

We'll open this door and start walking across the arena. They may not realize we are escaping until we are close to the door."

"You guards need to go elsewhere and quickly," said the Artobas headman. "Don't be anywhere around here when we make our break! Go now!"

The four warriors turned and left at a run.

"Ki-Gor!" came a distant call. "Ki-Gor, is that you?"

"That sounded like Katonga," exclaimed Ki-Gor. "I'll check!"

The two men kept talking to each other and it only took the jungle man seconds to locate the cell that contained Katonga. With him was Meca Huko!

"What happened?" asked Ki-Gor, as he simply gripped the bars of the cell door and ripped them away.

"The Queen, Meca Huko's sister," said Katonga as they joined Ki-Gor in the hallway, "decided she wanted the two pale boys to be her slaves. Meca Huko, and others, tried to reason with her that they had only been brought here for treatment. Both had been bitten by the Gyjak they were teasing. The bite is poisonous, but it takes a little time to work. Meca Huko brought them here and they were treated and then all three were imprisoned."

"How did you end up in the cell?" asked Ki-Gor.

"I went to the Queen asking that Meca Huko be freed along with the boys as it is against our laws to do what she was doing," Katonga replied with a shake of his head.

"Your laws?" asked Helene, as they were now back with the group.

"Yes," nodded Katonga. "I am originally from Tobonglan. Also, Meca Huko is the Queen's twin sister! They are the only known twins to be born in our country!"

"We are going through the arena," said Ki-Gor, "and out the far door onto the shelf. Can you direct us to the Smoking Cavern from there?"

"Yes," nodded Katonga, who was looking through a crack in the slightly opened door to view the arena. "And we had better be making our break, as the stands are filling up! We don't want too many spectators watching us!"

"Do you have any weapons?" asked Ki-Gor, looking at Katonga and Meca Huko. "Motribo and Laketna are both armed. So is Helene. They did not take our weapons as we were supposed to be just visitors, I think."

"No," said Katonga, shaking his head. "They took our weapons immediately. Meca Huko because she is the Queen's sister and, therefore, considered a threat. Me, because I came looking for her and the boys."

Ki-Gor nodded and handed Katonga his assegai. "I have this sword that attracted so much attention from the Queen," he commented. "I will use it!"

Helene was watching Ki-Gor and when he gave the warrior his assegai, she turned and offered her weapon to Meca Huko.

"Thank you," replied the twin sister of the Queen and she spoke in English.

"You are welcome, my friend," replied Helene.

"What will you use?" asked Katonga. "Your belt knife? That won't do much good, although it will be better than nothing."

Helene smiled. "I still have Gabe Jacobson's hand gun," she replied. "I will not use it until it becomes absolutely necessary, but I can and will use it if I need to!"

"We will walk out as though we are going across the arena for some reason," said Ki-Gor. "perhaps they will not notice anything is wrong."

The group opened the door and moved into the arena. They stopped while the door was closed and then Motribo, Katonga, Laketna and Meca Huko formed a guard around Ki-Gor, Helene and the two boys as though they being escorted somewhere.

Things went smoothly and the group was halfway to the tunnel leading to the outside when the Queen entered the royal box and seated herself with her attendants. The first thing she noticed was the departure of the prisoners that were to provide the entertainment. She sat perplexed for a few seconds. Then she leaped to her feet, screaming.

"They are getting away!" she yelped. "Stop them! Release the beasts! Stop them immediately! Turn loose the beasts!" she screeched again.

The arena was not a large place and the Queen could be heard easily all through the area. Suddenly a door was slammed back against the wall amid heavy growling and barking. Flowing into the enclosure was a pack of six vicious dog-like creatures. They were not too dissimilar from the dog-like animals the beast-men had been riding.

The escaping group formed a circle facing the creatures and continued to back toward the door that would release them from the arena.

"Do not throw your spears," said Motribo. "Once you throw it, you are unarmed! Drive it home when they are close!"

Suddenly Helene stepped out in front of the group, facing the charging beasts. She leveled the hand gun and when the slavering animals were almost upon them, she easily shot the leading two dogs. The sound of the shots reverberated through the arena, causing dismay and concern among the spectators.

Helene was a good shot as she had practiced much in the past. Her first two shots rolled the two leaders in the dirt. Then she took down a third beast, leaving three who did not seem to know they were facing death.

Ki-Gor stepped in on the left and ran his jeweled sword through a fourth one with help from Laketna and her spear. On the right, Katonga and Motribo transfixed the fifth creature.

The one trailing, being a little slower and the sixth animal, drew Helene's attention. She turned slightly and fired just as Meca Huko's assegai rammed into the dog's rib cage. It was almost a point blank shot, but the dog buckled just as she pulled the trigger and the shot passed a few inches over the beast's head.

The Queen, across the arena, was standing, waving her arms and screaming orders that no one seemed to hear. Suddenly, she became quiet and slumped back into her seat. She sat quietly, her head lolled to one side with a small round hole in the center of the forehead. Blood oozed out and slowly ran down the side of her head.

The group in the arena moved quickly to the exit door. Ki-Gor lifted the huge bar that was intended for two men on each end to remove. Katonga pulled the door open and they were soon outside in the short tunnel.

Katonga and Motribo were pulling the gate closed when they first hear the cry from the spectators.

"The Queen is dead! The Queen is dead!"

"Is there a way to fasten this gate from the outside?" asked Ki-Gor.

"There is," said Motribo, "but it takes some time to get everything into place to actually lock the door. And if those fellows inside have any sense, they'll just pick up that log bar you removed, use it as a battering ram and be through in a very short time."

"We're better off to get farther away right now," said Katonga. "We can put more distance between us and our pursuers."

"You lead, Meca Huko," said Katonga. "Then Helene and the two boys. The rest of us will bring up the rear in case we actually have anyone getting close to us!"

The ledge leading away from the tunnel and exit door from the arena was wide and easy to traverse. In moments the large group was out of sight of the tunnel and moving rapidly.

The ledge went for a quarter of a mile and then began a long descent which eventually came to ground level. There had been no sign or sound of anyone following them.

"How far to the Smoking Caverns?" asked Ki-Gor once they had entered the jungle.

…the shot passed…over the beast's head.

"Several miles," said Katonga. "Let us move a short distance from here," he added. "That will make it difficult on any group trying to follow us from the arena. Then we need to stop and plan what we are going to do."

The group, led by Katonga and Motribo, continued through the jungle following a trail that was not very visible. However, after eight people had gone over it, the trail was quite visible to anyone wanting to follow it.

It was very late in the afternoon, when the group came to a stop. The two youngsters were totally exhausted.

They started a fire and sat down to rest.

"The door to the Smoking Cavern is a couple of hundred steps from here," said Katonga. "However, as Motribo and I were closing the arena door, we heard the crowd shouting and I am sure they were saying, 'The Queen is dead! The Queen is dead!' Perhaps the excitement of her prisoners escaping was too much for her and she collapsed."

"Or, perhaps an assassin took this opportunity of confusion," said Motribo, "to slip a blade between her ribs. Whatever happened, we think Meca Huko's sister is gone. You know what that means," he added, looking at the seated Artobas.

"Yes," said Katonga. "That means that Meca Huko should ascend to the throne."

The woman's face was emotionless and then tears began to roll down her cheeks. "She had me in prison," Meca Huko said softly, "but I do not think she meant me harm. She has always known that I have no interest in ruling. That I was never a threat to her!"

"I believe," said Katonga, "the Queen harbored suspicions that I might be wanting the throne and would be using Meca Huko to get it. But, I am like my mate," he added, looking at the tall beautiful woman crying, "I have no interest in ruling people."

"You and Meca Huko are mates!" exclaimed Helene. "I had just decided that you were all from the Artobas tribe, but..."

"Yes, we are mated," smiled Katonga. "We have been for over forty years. Since our tribe no longer does the mating thing, we did it on the other side of the mountains."

"You were mates before Ki-Gor or I were born!" exclaimed Helene.

They discussed their situation for a few minutes longer, then Meca Huko dried her eyes and spoke. "I believe it is my duty to return to Vaskin," she said. "I should be there for the arrangements for my sister. Also, the people of Tobonglan need to know I am here and available. Although ruling is something I am not interested in doing. Having been on the outside,

I believe there is much Katonga and I can do for the welfare of our people."

"It is not good to go through the Smoking Cavern during the night hours," said Katonga, "and it will soon be dark. I should return to the other side with Ki-Gor, Helene and the boys. I should also see to it that Gabe Jacobson returns safely to the coast. We can go to the other side as soon as it is light tomorrow."

"Then Laketna and I should return with Meca Huko to Vaskin," said Motribo. "I have people waiting there for me. And Laketna and I can act as body guards for the new Queen."

"Can we leave now?" asked Meca Huko.

"Yes," nodded Motribo.

Katonga and Motribo stood up and faced each other. Both men were smiling. As they stood there, Helene could see the distinct likeness between the two men. She wondered if they were brothers or perhaps half-brothers, but they would not know.

"I will stay here," Katonga was saying, "then I will see that our friends get through the caverns and back to Gabe Jacobson's camp. He is my responsibility, so I will see to it that he arrives at the coast in safety. Then I shall return here."

"You are a good man, Katonga," said Motribo. "I will accompany Meca Huko back to Vaskin. There, I and my warriors, will remain until all is settled. We may still be there when you return. Or we may have returned to our village."

Ki-Gor and Helene watched with the two boys and Katonga as Motribo and the two women began the return journey to Vaskin.

M'Gutu was in poor spirits as were the two men accompanying him. The rain came and forced the men to find shelter. This they did. They stayed holed up until the following day when the rain finally came to a stop.

Both Ndota and Tguffo were hungry and they set out to hunt, regardless of the dislike exhibited by M'Gutu. The hunt dragged on and finally a small antelope was brought down. They dressed out the creature right on the spot where they had made their kill. A fire pit was dug and they soon had the skinned carcass spitted and roasting over hot burning low flames.

Then when the meat was done to the point where the men would eat it, which was still fairly raw, they gorged themselves. Once finished with the meal, they lay back with full stomachs to rest and it was late in the day before M'Gutu could get them on their feet and moving again.

When they finally reached the Ieka River and looked over the bluff, they saw a wide expanse of water. The rains in the Shikashika Mountains were now flooding the river and the sand bar where the white man was rumored to be camped was all under water.

"You lazy dogs!" he railed at his two friends. "Because of you my children will be turned into mice and my woman into a cat!"

"M'Gutu," said Ndota, "that all sounds like a plan."

"What plan?" demanded the distraught man.

"Oh, my friend, you are so easily duped!" cackled Ndota. "T'Chuka wants the blood of a white man. You are summoned and you must accept the responsibility of getting this white man. As you know, Chief Magawa's daughter has her eyes on you, my friend."

"No, I did not know!" snapped M'Gutu. "I am a married man, with a family! I have no interest in the Chief's daughter! That would be a good way to end your life early!"

"Huh!" grunted Tguffo, "Every one in the village knows! Your woman knows, for sure! She has enough friends telling her!"

"What!" exclaimed M'Gutu. "This is not so!"

"My friend," said Ndota, "Chief Magawa's daughter, Nene, was to follow you out here on your trek for the white man that does not exist. Tguffo and I were to slip away upon her arrival and leave the two of you alone! Hee, hee!"

"The rain must have washed her ardor away!" giggled Tguffo.

"Or the *kingugwa* got her," said M'Gutu. "Or perhaps the *kifaru*! Or *simba*!"

"You should hope not," said Ndota. "You know who the Chief will hold responsible!"

As the three warriors argued and gazed across the river, a spiral of smoke wound lazily upward.

"There!" exclaimed M'Gutu. "That is the white man's fire! See, he just moved up the slope away from the flooding waters! Ha! I will get him now!"

"But how are you going to cross the flooded river?" asked Tguffo.

"I have two friends that I brought along just for that purpose," chortled M'Gutu. "We will find downed trees washed up along the flooded river bank! We will lash them together and float across!"

"Then we should go far upstream so we can float with the current," said Ndota.

The three men did as they planned and by darkness they were pushing their makeshift raft onto the bank below the slope where they had seen the smoke earlier.

Carefully they moved up the slope, stopping often to listen and moving as silent as the wind. Finally, they were rewarded with the white man's camp and the lone occupant dozing peacefully in his chair before his tent.

The men entered the camp, walked silently up to the sleeping man, thumped him on the head and carried him back to the river. Soon they were working their way across the flooded waters to the opposite side.

When they finally beached on the opposite side, they were at least half a mile below their starting point.

Jacobson had regained consciousness somewhere midway across the Ieka and when he realized he was floating on three trunks fastened haphazardly together, he was frightened. He was too scared to talk, but when they landed on the west bank of the river, his bravado returned and he began to harangue his captors.

Immediately, he was thrown to the ground and his hands tied behind his back. Then a rope was placed around his neck and each time he began to berate his captors, they simply jerked on the rope until Gabe Jacobson had a raw and bloody neck. He was suffering from so much pain, that he finally saw the wisdom in remaining quiet.

When Helene awoke the following morning, she was surprised to look up and see two moons floating in the night sky. At first, she thought she was dreaming. The moon she was used to seeing was in the western sky. But in the east was another moon. It was much smaller than the first moon and appeared to be a long distance away but, Helene knew, that was all a matter of perspective.

"Ki-Gor," she whispered urgently, "wake up!"

The white man rolled over and sat up. He was near the fire that had been kept burning throughout the night for the warmth. Helene was on one side of him while Jerry and Ray were on the opposite side. Across the fire was Katonga, who had kept it burning during the dark hours.

"Good morning, Helene," the man said. "Did you sleep well?"

"Yes," his mate replied, "considering it was chilly and the ground was hard!"

The man chuckled lightly.

"Look up there," she pointed. "There are two moons in the sky! We can't be on Earth!"

"Helene," said Katonga from his position across the fire, "you are on Earth. Take a close look at the moon in the west. It is the same one you see on your side of the mountains, is it not?"

"Yes," nodded the woman, "the marking are all the same."

"On this side of the mountains," the man continued, "we are in a different time. Perhaps thousands and thousands of years earlier. We have animals living here that on your side of the mountains are only bones in your museums. At that early time, there must have been two moons circling the Earth. That you can see for yourself."

"But what happened to the smaller one?" she asked.

Katonga chuckled. "We do not know the answer to that," he replied. "Sometime, between here and there," he said, "something happened to it. Only a few of us are even aware that a second moon ever existed."

"Let us eat," said Ki-Gor. "I am anxious to get Jerry and Ray back to their father. I am sure he is quite worried about their safety."

The jungle man was warming up some of the meat they had cooked the previous evening after a short hunt. Also, there was a good supply of edible fruit they had gathered. Jerry and Ray had been hungry for the evening meal and they were equally hungry for breakfast.

"They are growing boys," said Helene when Ki-Gor commented on how much they had eaten. "They take a lot of food."

When they arrived at the doorway into the Smoking Cavern, both Ki-Gor and Helene realized it was not the door through which they had entered this strange world.

"There are six different doorways leading into the burial chambers," explained Katonga.

Helene was lighting torches with her matches. "Why couldn't we have just lit torches last night and walked on through to the other side?" she asked.

"And have you miss the two moons of my world?" the man laughed.

"No, seriously, why couldn't we have gone through last night? We could have had Jerry and Ray back with their father by now."

"It is said," replied Katonga in a serious voice, "the spirits of those interred in the caverns move about during the night hours. One does not want to be in the caverns at that time."

They had lit two torches and Katonga took one leading the way. They walked past rooms with the life-like figures waiting motionlessly. They talked in low tones as they advanced and it was not long before they opened a door and stepped out of the Smoking Caverns.

"Oh!" exclaimed Helene, "the sun is more yellow! It is not as red as it was in Tobonglan. It is good to be back."

"I shall whistle," said Ki-Gor, "and see if Marmo is in the area. We might as well ride, if we can."

The jungle man turned and climbed up a small knoll where he gave a long, shrill, undulating whistle. He waited a short bit and then repeated it. Then Ki-Gor rejoined his group and they started the trek toward Gabe Jacobson's camp.

They had not gone far when a dark shape emerged from the jungle. Both Jerry and Ray cried out in fear as they had never seen anything so huge. Even Katonga stepped back, leaving Ki-Gor and Helene to meet their friend.

After several minutes of talking and rubbing the big elephant, the beast wrapped his trunk lightly about Helene and lifted her to his back. Then Ki-Gor had him place Katonga up on his back. When it was time for Jerry and Ray to be lifted, they refused to come close to the elephant.

"This much easier than walking," said Ki-Gor, but both boys were adamant about not being lifted onto the animal's back with Helene and Katonga.

"Then follow along behind," said Ki-Gor. "If you get tired and want to ride, just call out and we will get you on board."

Jerry and Ray followed Marmo all the way to the camp of Gabe Jacobson.

"Hey, this isn't where Dad wanted his camp," exclaimed Jerry as they walked into the area where the tent was pitched.

"And where is Dad?" asked Ray, a tremor of nervousness in his voice.

Ki-Gor and Katonga both slid quickly to the ground as they realized there did not seem to be anyone in camp. It did not take long to determine the camp was deserted.

Helene dismounted with Marmo's help and went into the tent where she reloaded her handgun from Gabe's supplies. She also found a small sack which she filled with shells and tied to her belt.

The two men quickly picked up the trail of M'Gutu and his friends and it was easy to read the sign that Gabe Jacobson had been drug to the edge of the river.

"They have crossed to the other side," said Katonga. "You boys now have a choice," he said, turning to Jerry and Ray. "You can either get on the elephant and cross the river with us as we search for your father or you can go back to the camp and wait until we return. But I'll tell you one thing, boys, if you are not there when we return, we are not going out looking for you!"

Reluctantly, the two boys let Ki-Gor lift them up and push them toward Helene who caught them and pulled them onto the back of the elephant. Then Marmo lifted first Katonga and then Ki-Gor onto his back and they started into the flowing muddy water of the Ieka River.

Ki-Gor knew the location of the village from which the three warriors came and they made no attempt to follow a trail but just moved out in that direction.

It was midday when they began to hear the sound of the drums. Ki-Gor spoke soothingly to the big elephant and they continued toward the village.

"We do not know what we will see when we enter the village," Ki-Gor said to the two boys. "Do not dismount! Remain on Marmo!"

"Do you understand the jungle drums?" asked Katonga. "It is something I was never good at deciphering."

"I am not as good as some," Ki-Gor replied, "but I do know they have a prisoner and that he is being tortured. That might be good in that it means he is still alive. But he could be alive and be beyond all hope of recovering."

"Do you have a plan?" Katonga asked.

"I don't think we have much time," said Ki-Gor. "I will just take Marmo right into the village and see what happens. Most natives are somewhat afraid of a mad elephant and they don't know the difference in a trumpeting one entering their village and a mad one! I will have Marmo making a lot of noise."

"There, you can see the village," exclaimed Helene, pointing. "There is a lot of smoke coming up, so they are burning something!"

Ki-Gor gigged Marmo with his heels, urging the elephant to go faster. Sensing the urgency of the situation, the elephant began trumpeting as he neared the village. The drumming came to a stop. The huge pachyderm pushed right through the log stockade surrounding the village.

Ki-Gor gave a thundering bellow that made the hair on the backs of Jerry's and Ray's necks stand on end. Then they saw their father.

Gabe Jacobson was in bad shape. He was tied between two poles set in the center of the village and in front of his bound feet was a blazing fire, just waiting to be pushed up against him. His body was covered with blood from dozens of small knife and spear pricks.

Old T'Chuka sat near the white man, his face covered with blood. He had collected some of the white man's blood and mixed his potion. Now he would survive for many more years. He was pleased with himself until he saw the gigantic elephant thundering toward him. He leaped up and ran screaming, plowing right into Chief Magawa. Both men tumbled to the ground.

"You!" exclaimed the leader, recognizing the odor before he saw the little sorcerer. "Do something! Stop that beast! Change him into a mouse!"

The fellow scrambled to his feet and the old chief poked the sorcerer with his spear point to help him along with his magic. Fleeing from the spear, T'Chuka ran directly toward Marmo's swinging trunk. The elephant swatted the aged sorcerer and the fellow tumbled into the fire burning in front of the bound prisoner. The witch doctor's greasy rags ignited in something just short of an explosion. He came barreling out of the fire, screeching, and raced toward his hut, flames streaming out behind him. His stringy white hair was totally missing. In moments the sorcerer's domicile was a ball of fire. The screaming stopped.

There was not a man, woman or child left in the village as Ki-Gor slid to the ground. He pulled out his knife and hurried to the bound Gabe Jacobson where he freed the man from his bonds. The fellow was still conscious and groaning from the inflicted pain he had suffered as Ki-Gor picked him up and carried him away from the fire.

Katonga brought a vessel of water standing by a nearby hut and they washed the man down with the cooling liquid.

Ki-Gor sent Jerry and Ray to search the huts for a blanket on which they could place their father. They were soon back with one.

The Jungle Lord was sure the Salgubas and their chief, Magawa, had not gone far and were hiding in the jungle, waiting for the intruders and their elephant to leave. He walked a short distance in the direction of the jungle, cupped his hands to his mouth and called to the chief.

"Chief Magawa!" he shouted. "I will burn every hut in your village, unless you help me! Come out now and we will talk!"

Shortly, the angry chief appeared and walked slowly toward Ki-Gor.

"I need you and three of your warriors to grab the corners of that blanket and carry it to the Ieka River!" said the Jungle Lord. "For that help, I will not burn your village to the ground. Once we arrive at the river you will be free to return!"

Chief Magawa turned and bellowed for M'Gutu, Ndota and Tguffo as they were the ones who had brought the accursed white man into their village.

A day later Ki-Gor and his group had returned to Gabe Jacobson's camp on the Ieka River. The man was resting and they felt he was recuperating well. Katonga was going to wait a few more days before he started toward the coast.

Ki-Gor and Helene came to say good-bye to the man and his sons before they departed.

"Thank you again for everything you've done for me and my boys!" Gabe said, reclining on his cot. "We will never forget you, Ki-Gor and Helene! But, wait, there is something I want to give to Helene! I believe you still have my pistol and I want you to keep it! But, I also want to give you all the ammunition I have for it! The boys told me about you shooting all those wild things in the arena, so you deserve it all!"

The Jungle Lord and his mate waved as they rode Marmo out of the white man's camp. Katonga, Gabe, Jerry and Ray all waved in return.

"One thing about it," said Helene with a giggle, "Gabe Jacobson has now seen a large African animal!"

THE END

TEMBU GEORGE AND THE SLAVERS

Col. Klaus Knappe slapped the desk top and stood up, a scowl covering his rugged face as he glared at the map on his desk. He had just started to utter an oath of profanity when the door opened and a young man walked into the room. The Colonel looked up to see the fellow smiling at him.

Manfred Wilhelm and Colonel Knappe quickly exchanged the mandatory *Sieg Heil* salute.

"What brings you here?" asked the Colonel. "Is there something I can help you with?"

"You look tired," replied Manfred before he answered the officer's question. "I am here because my wife, your niece, has been wanting me to stop by. Just to see how you are getting along, I believe."

Klaus Knappe grunted and moved toward the large window looking over the city of Berlin from his fifth floor office. He stood there, hands folded behind his back, staring outward. His nephew, by marriage, came to stand beside him.

"I am tired," he said softly. "However, now is not the time to think of retirement."

"I would agree," said Manfred.

The two men stood silent for a few moments, each somewhat uncomfortable in the company of the other.

"Is there anything I can do to help?" the younger man finally asked.

"No," said the older man slowly, "unless you happen to know of a way to add some wealth to the coffers of the Nazi Regime. They are in dire need of funds to keep their movement marching forward. They claim that within weeks they will have added conquests that will fill out their requirements. But, I have spent my life serving Deutschland in the military and one thing I have learned is that you can never count on something being accomplished in the amount of time that is projected. Something always gets in the way!"

Manfred Wilhelm nodded. But he was trying to think of a quick way to achieve wealth. It would have to be something that could be taken by force, or stealth.

The two men were again quiet for a length of time.

Finally, Manfred cleared his throat. "I remember hearing something about a high class Britisher in Africa who had discovered fabulous wealth on his holdings, or something like that, but I know very little about it. It probably isn't even true, but I do believe I read it in a newspaper a while back."

Klaus Knappe turned and looked hard at the young man, his blue eyes cold and glittering.

"You have heard of this?" he asked.

"Just what I have said," replied Wilhelm, "nothing more."

"Do you believe it?"

"I don't think so," Manfred stuttered slightly. "It sounds like a story made up to gain readers. I really have my doubts!"

"But, if it is true," said Colonel Knappe, "we really should check it out. If there is wealth located on some Britisher's holdings in Africa, shouldn't we deserve it as much as he?"

Manfred Wilhelm nodded slightly. "However, if the regime is short on funds, how can they afford to send an expedition into British East Africa?"

The Colonel smiled an almost wicked smile. "They can come up with funds when they want to," he grumbled.

Manfred nodded as he had suspected as much, but would not say so verbally.

"Come over here," said Colonel Knappe, moving toward his desk. "I want to show you something."

Manfred Wilhelm was stunned when he looked down at the map spread out on Colonel Knappe's desk. It was a map of Africa extending from south of the equator north to the Mediterranean Sea. There were several pencil markings in the area labeled British East Africa.

"What?" he exclaimed. "You were already looking at the situation I brought up! What do you know about this?"

"That is what I want to ask you," smiled Colonel Knappe. "Did you, by any chance, happen to see the map on my desk before you mentioned the Britisher?"

"Not at all," replied Manfred. "In fact, I can show you the newspaper from which I read the article. I am sure it is still in the apartment."

"I'd like to see that," nodded the colonel.

"I take it," said Manfred slowly, "that you have sources much more knowledgeable on this subject than I am?"

The older man nodded. "This area right here," he said, tapping his finger on the map, "is a huge expanse covering thousands of square miles! It is larger than many countries! And I don't mean those small places that are too tiny to get on a map! This chunk of mountainous, jungle covered land is enormous. Almost anything could be hiding in there. Wealth, which we desperately need, could be there for all we know. The question is, should we take the time and effort to send an expedition?"

"If you were to send a military expedition," said Manfred, "it could be construed as an invasion. Is that something our leaders want at this time?"

"No, I think not," replied Colonel Knappe. "But I do think it is essential we check out the possibility of wealth hidden there. Something like gold mines or diamonds or the burial grounds of some of those ancient kings."

Manfred nodded. "It needs to be something that can be brought out in small amounts. Perhaps carried by safari porters and such."

"And it has to be done by trustworthy individuals," the Colonel said. "We don't want to draw attention to what we are doing or looking for, but those in charge must be totally dependable."

"I'm not seeing much in the way of towns and roads," said Manfred, bending over and looking at the area on the map. "Perhaps they just haven't been recorded."

"I think," said the Colonel with a slight smile, "that such is non-existent. The area is very much untamed and not many white men have ever set foot there."

"You believe this is where that wealthy English Lord has his estate? The area where he has found added wealth?"

"Not me so much, as the others involved in this. I'm a little reluctant to actually believe there is something out there and that we can find it, if it is." The colonel walked back to stare out the window.

"Much of that," said Manfred, "will depend on your man in charge. I am assuming you will send a military man, posing as a civilian, of course. I could give you a couple of recommendations, if you want."

"I think," said Colonel Knappe, "that our superiors have already made a decision on who they want to send. And I am not at liberty to say at this time," he added.

Manfred nodded.

"Were you thinking about perhaps applying for the assignment?" his uncle asked.

"No, not really," the young man said. "I haven't had that much time to think about it."

"Umm," nodded the older man. "Another thing I've learned, in addition to not being able to tell when a job will be completed, is not to think you know what your superiors will decide. It will invariably be wrong! Sometimes I think they change things just to make you wrong!"

Manfred chuckled and the Colonel joined him.

"Manfred," said Colonel Knappe, turning to the man by his side, "I do not know you very well. Only that you married my niece a few months back."

"Just eight months ago," Manfred interjected a smile on his face.

"Oh, yes," the man nodded. "I believe I did hear, though, that you had been to Africa before you married my niece. Have you been there?"

Manfred nodded, without elaborating.

"Good. Fine," the Colonel said.

"If there is nothing I can do for you," said the younger man, "I really should be moving along."

"Nice of you to stop by," Klaus Knappe said as they saluted each other.

That evening Manfred Wilhelm looked for the paper in which he had read the story about the British Lord and his discovery of wealth. The newspaper was nowhere to be found. All the papers preceding it and all those following it were there. But the one he wanted was missing.

When he and his wife, Heidi, were seated at the small table for their evening meal, he mentioned the missing paper.

"Sweetheart," said his wife, with a soft glow in her blue eyes, "it was a newspaper. Anything can happen to a newspaper. If there was something you wanted, perhaps we could pick one up from a neighbor."

"I don't think any of our neighbors get the paper," he said.

"You are probably right," Heidi agreed, reaching up to brush back a lock of her short blonde hair. "Is it important enough that we should go to the newspaper plant and buy another copy?"

"Oh, no," he replied quickly. "It was nothing really. If I recall correctly, the story was based on an article that originally appeared in a Paris paper."

Heidi smiled and nodded, as her husband admired the slim tall form of his wife.

"I stopped by and saw your Uncle Knappe today," Manfred said. "He seems to be fine, although he did admit to being tired. He should be looking at retirement, but that can't happen with the current political situation."

"Did he say anything important?" asked Heidi as she washed the few dishes they had used. "Like anything exciting going on?"

"No, not really," her husband replied. "But you know how it is in the military. Everyone has to be very careful not to say the wrong thing! You are so lucky to be working outside of the military. Your boss may send you on a few road trips, but at least it doesn't have anything to do with all the intrigue that goes on around me! There are times I really wonder if I can make it to the point of pulling a decent salary and being able to eventually retire."

"We are both far too young to be thinking of retirement," said his wife.

Manfred nodded a tired look on his face. "I'd kind of like to leave the service and get a civilian job, but, as you know, that is out of the question!"

"Absolutely," agreed Heidi. "You know that many of the people who leave the service, for one reason or another, often disappear or become a fatality in an accident! You do not want to take that chance!"

"Of course not," agreed Manfred.

"You mentioned my boss sending me on business trips for his company. He informed me today that I might be leaving on another one soon. He didn't say just where or what the purpose was, but I am to be ready."

Manfred gave a long drawn out sigh which was not lost on his wife.

Tembu George returned late in the day to his tribe of M'Balla Masai. The red sun in the west was sinking rapidly and he was ready to call it a day. He wanted nothing more than a good meal and then time to sit and visit with Shaliba, his wife. He had many things to tell her as he had been gone for close to a week.

George Spelvin of Cincinnati was a tall man towering in the neighborhood of six and a half feet in height. However, he was still on the short end of the stick when compared to his Masai warriors who stood just above seven feet on the average. While the Masai were long and lean, George was muscled out much more than they were.

George had arrived at the M'Balla village at a ground eating trot, but he slowed his approach to a long striding walk as he entered the settlement consisting of straw huts plastered together with mud. The women of the tribe in constructing the dwellings covered them with a mud mixture that actually shed the rainfall very nicely.

As the M'Balla chieftain approached his home, he thought it was unusual that he could see no light, either from a cooking fire or from an inside fire that would keep away the night chill. He had just started to break into a run when he heard a voice calling him and turned to see his wife's sister hurrying toward him.

"Tembu George!" she exclaimed. "I have been watching for you! I sent runners to find you, but no one knew just where to look for you!"

"What happened?" the man asked abruptly.

"It is Shaliba," said the woman, her voice shaking. "She left four days ago to see the man who lives in the Sandy Gorge. You know the place. Someone came in and told her he had heard loud crying in that gorge! He tried to find the source, but whoever was making the noise must have seen him as they stopped and he could not find them. He called many times. When he returned to the village, he told Shaliba what he had heard since you were not here."

"Who was this man?" asked Tembu George.

"Otchkina," the woman replied. "He is now out with a party of men who are chasing some cow thieves!"

"And Shaliba decided to check on the man and his wife who live alone in the Sandy Gorge, is that right?"

"Yes, she thought there wasn't time to wait for you to get back. Especially if someone had been hurt or needed help. She and two of our sisters left for the gorge, but they should have returned at least two days ago! Something must have happened to them!"

"I shall go now," said Tembu George. "I will pick up some dried food, gather ten warriors and be gone before the sun is completely down!"

The war chief of the M'Balla Masai went into his straw home and returned in just less than a minute. He carried a pouch in one hand and went immediately to a nearby hut and before another three minutes had passed, Tembu George was going out the village gate with ten stalwart warriors trailing in his wake. Each man carried a large shield and a long, heavy spear with a two foot blade. In addition, each man carried a long knife strapped about his waist and a pouch of trail food. Several also carried a bow and quiver of arrows across their backs.

In addition, Tembu George had a pistol strapped about his waist with a cartridge belt containing extra rounds. Over his shoulder was a large caliber rifle. He had acquired the weapons a few weeks earlier when he and Ki-Gor had confronted a safari intent on killing any wildlife they could set their sights on. It was a small group, but when they realized they were just facing a white man gone native and a black Hercules, they decided it might be fun to shoot it out! As soon as the safari opened fire, Ki-Gor and Tembu George just disappeared. Much ammunition was expended and the glade was soon filled with the acrid smell of gun smoke. But presently the lone remaining white man realized he was surrounded by the dead bodies of his comrades and there was still no sign of the white man and black man. The fellow lowered his gun and looked around in amazement. It seemed that every body had an arrow protruding from it. The surviving man at first felt anger and that was soon replaced with a feeling of fear. Then he was facing the big black man. Instantly he raised his pistol and pulled the trigger. The hammer fell on an empty shell as a large black hand clamped on the hand gun and forced it upward. The man fell backwards, jerking the pistol away from Tembu George. Then he threw the gun at the advancing warrior and began clawing his knife from his belt. He was screaming obscenities as he charged forward. Then he felt the two foot long blade of the spear sliding through his chest. There was a sharp pain and then darkness.

Tembu George became the owner of several firearms that day, two of which he carried with him as he led his Masai toward Sandy Gorge.

Darkness came quickly. However, it wasn't long before a bright moon gave light to the fast moving contingent heading toward Sandy Gorge. While they had no trouble seeing well enough to make rapid travel possible, there simply wasn't enough light to follow any kind of spoor the three women might have left four days earlier. George wasted no time in trying to find something that would not be there.

The ten Masai and Tembu George moved through the jungle and the open areas like dark shadows. Other than the sound of heavy breathing, they made little or no noise.

It was past midnight when they stopped near the edge of the drop off that marked the side of the gorge. They stood silently listening. Several of the men, including Tembu George, were also trying to pick up any scent that might be on the light breeze coming up from the ravine.

After a few moments, the Masai moved toward a break in the wall where a trail led down into the gorge. The surface of the path was sandy and showed a great number of tracks in the moonlight, all of which were left by animals using the trail in recent days. Tembu George and several of his followers dropped to the ground and spent a few moments trying to pick up the scent of something that did not belong there.

"Huh," the M'Balla chief grunted softly. "It is faint, but I think I smell men who should not have been here." He looked questioningly at the men who had been checking for a scent with him. Two of them nodded with a grim look on their faces. They, too, had caught the faint odor of strangers.

"What do you think?" Tembu George asked.

"A native smell would have been gone by this time," said one of the men. "Only the stink of a slaver would linger so long."

The other man nodded, as did Tembu George.

"We shall go to the cave of the loner," said the leader, "and see what we can learn there!"

In single file, they fell in behind Tembu George and entered Sandy Gorge.

The gorge, itself, was perhaps a quarter of a mile wide and ran for approximately two miles before fading away. At some point, perhaps thousands of years ago, the gorge had carried a tremendous amount of water that had caused the very sandy surface now.

Along this wall of the Sandy Gorge, there were two trails giving easy access to the wash area. Tembu George and his men had used the south one. There was a north entrance just over a mile farther along the edge.

The Masai had not covered more than a quarter of a mile when the trailing warrior gave a shrill bird call that brought the entire contingent to a stop, whirling with spears at the ready to face the rear. Coming out of the vegetation not far from the trail was a water buffalo. They were not too often seen in this area, but it was not unheard of, and this fellow seemed to be upset that his rest had been disturbed.

The bull came to a stop, blew through his nostrils and pawed the ground. The Masai quickly formed a semi-circle and waited for the fellow to make up his mind if he was going to charge or go back into the jungle darkness.

With a deep bawl, the buffalo suddenly lurched forward, head lowered. The Masai he faced nimbly avoided him while several of the others within reach impaled the bull with their iron shod spears. Out of the eleven warriors, six of them had rammed home their blade. The creature staggered and then turned ready to charge again. Then came the heavy echoing boom of the big gun Tembu George was carrying and a large hole appeared in the animal's forehead. The frothing beast went to his knees, then with a labored bawl, rolled over on his side, dying.

"It is a shame to not be able to take the meat," said one of the men.

"Bleed him," said Tembu George. "Perhaps the loner or his woman can come out and butcher him with the sunrise."

Within minutes the Masai and their chief were moving again. Otchkina, the warrior who had heard the cries a few days earlier, was not aware of the location of the loner's cave. However, Tembu George knew exactly where to find it.

Soon they were within sight of the dark cave located far above the bed of the ravine. They stopped and the M'Balla chieftain cupped his hands to his mouth and shouted upward.

"Othoya!" he called loudly. "Tembu George is here to see you! Othoya, come out immediately. We have much to say!"

The cave remained silent, although Muwari, the chief's second in command, thought he saw a movement in the shadows.

"Othoya," Tembu George called again. "This is your friend, Tembu George! We have come far to see you!"

There was still silence.

"Nomul, we are here to help you! Would you come out and visit with us?" Tembu George hesitated, and then added, "We have fresh food for you!"

"Tembu George?" came a plaintive voice, "is it really you? I heard the gun and thought the slavers might have returned."

A figure appeared in the front of the cave and the Masai chief waved his arm at the woman. "Yes," he replied. "We are here to help you and Othoya. Come down so we may talk."

As the men watched, a knotted rope made of braided strips of animal skins was tossed over the edge and the woman, Nomul, began coming down the side.

She seemed hesitant when her feet were finally on the ground but once she had determined that it was, indeed, Tembu George, she came forward with a big smile on her face.

"What brings you to the Sandy Gorge?" she asked softly. "Othoya is not here now. Is there something I may do for you?"

"Perhaps," smiled Tembu George. "About six days ago a Masai warrior heard much crying here in the gorge. He tried to find the source, but to no avail. He did not know where to look for your cave. He returned to the Masai kraal and left a message with my wife, Shaliba. I was gone at the time, so my wife got two of her sisters and came out this way thinking they might be of some help if you were in trouble. They have not returned. We are here to see if you or your mate might know something about this?"

Tears were coursing down Nomul's cheeks. She was shaking her head, a frown on her face.

"Slavers!" she choked out and then began swallowing as she tried to continue speaking. "They came," she said after a moment. "They caught Othoya as he fought them off so I could escape! They hunted for me and I hid. Later, when they were gone, I cried! I screamed loudly, wishing I could die!"

Tembu George placed his two big hands on the woman's shoulders and smiled at her. "Nomul," he said, "slavers do not take prisoners to kill them. They take them to sell as slaves. Othoya is still alive out there somewhere!

We came searching for Shaliba and two of her sisters. If you have not seen them, there is a very strong possibility that they were also taken by these slavers."

"I have not seen them," replied Nomul. "I remember Shaliba and I think she knows where my cave is. She would have come there if she could have."

Tembu George nodded.

"How many slavers were there when your mate was taken?"

"Four slavers and two servants," said Nomul. "But they had guns!"

"Six of them are no match for the Masai!" exclaimed Muwari.

"Right," nodded Tembu George. "Are you hungry?" he asked, turning back to Nomul.

The woman nodded. "I have been afraid to leave the cave," she whispered. "I have not eaten for two days. I am beginning to feel hungry."

Tembu George chuckled. "We have plenty of food, just down the trail a short way. We had to kill a buffalo bull when we first came into the gorge. My warriors need to eat and rest until sunup. At that time we can pick up the trail and will be following the slavers. In the meantime, we will butcher the bull and leave you with plenty of meat. Can you salt it, dry it or smoke it to preserve it?"

Nomul smiled. "I can do all three," she said. "We have salt for that purpose."

The woman accompanied George and the Masai back to the slain buffalo. With all twelve of them working, it did not take overly long to remove the hide, which Nomul said she could use. Next they took the cuts of meat they wanted. The warriors carried a good portion of the beast back to the cave for Nomul. She climbed up to her cave and then pulled up the hide and meat the men had fastened to her rope.

"We will go to the north entrance," said Tembu George. "There we will eat and sleep until sun rise. Then we will pick up the trail and begin to run down those slavers!"

Nomul waved as the Masai warriors moved away from the area of the cave. Tembu George waved in return.

The Masai had eaten a small amount of the bloody meat raw as they butchered the animal, as that was their way. Tembu George, while he could and on occasion did eat raw meat, preferred his meat to be cooked somewhat.

They had brought one haunch with them and when they settled down for the night just a short distance from the northern entrance, the men began slicing off strips of the raw meat. Muwari and the men ate their portion raw, while Tembu George started a small fire and cooked his to suit his taste.

Once they had finished eating, the men went to the small stream that meandered through the gorge. There they washed away the smell of the blood that clung to their bodies from the butchering they had done.

They slept near the small fire Tembu George had used to cook his meat. It provided a scant amount of warmth and was also a deterrent to night prowlers.

With the dawn, Tembu George was up. He cooked and ate another strip of meat. Then Muwari joined him and the two men went over to the trail leading down from the edge of the gorge. Immediately they could detect the faint scent of the slavers.

They climbed to the rim of the gorge and again checked the area. They soon found where a scuffle of some sort had taken place. Here George and Muwari both picked up the scent of their women in addition to finding faint tracks that could have belonged to the Masai females.

They returned to the camp area and informed the remaining nine warriors of the situation. In a few short moments they had the area cleaned and the fire buried. Other than the faint odor of burned wood, there was little to show that someone had even been there.

Tembu George hit a ground eating lope with his warriors strung out right behind him.

The few hours rest had done wonders for them and they felt like they could run all day. And in all likelihood, they probably could have! However, George was cognizant of the fact that he needed his men fit to fight when the time came. They took short breaks every so often and drank water whenever it was available.

By mid afternoon, the trail seemed fresher. From the time the slavers had left the Sandy Gorge area, they had traveled unerringly to the northwest.

"My Chief," said Muwari as they jogged along, "how fast do you think we are gaining on those slavers?"

"Othoya, Shaliba and her two sisters are either shackled or bound," replied Tembu George. "Either way, they cannot travel fast. It is my thought that we have cut their lead in half by now."

"If we stay on this pace," said Muwari, "we might come upon their camp by midnight, do you think?"

"Yes, about that time," agreed Tembu George. "However, I do not want to have the men tired when we meet up with them. We may take a break

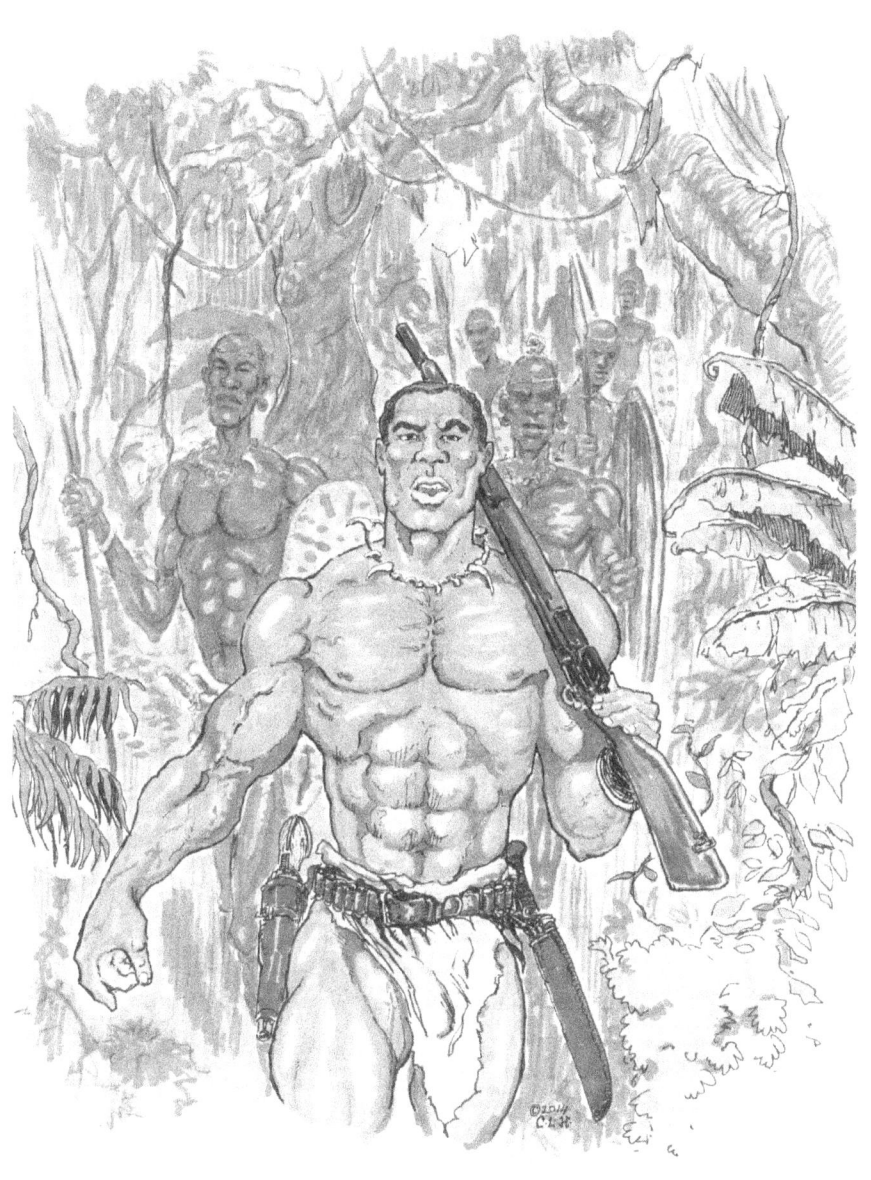

Tembu George hit a ground eating lope…

about sundown. Eat and rest. Then move on at a slower pace."

Muwari nodded and grinned.

A short time later Tembu George held up his arm and the group came to a halt. Then he, Muwari and a couple of other men knelt and looked at the ground. When they finally stood up, George looked at his sub chief. "What did you read?" he asked.

"I see where the first group was joined by a second group," Muwari replied. "I think six men on foot and three riding mules."

Tembu George looked at the other two men who had been down checking the sign left on the trail. Both nodded in agreement with the sub chief.

"I do not believe any were slaves," said George thoughtfully. "But they are traveling together now, so they must be of the same group."

"We are now facing a larger number," said Muwari.

"We will advance a little more slowly," said Tembu George. "I want to be strong, if we have to fight."

They were traveling through country covered with grass and many stands of jungle growth. The terrain was hilly which would slow the slavers much more than it would the Masai.

It was over an hour before sunset and the men had stopped at a creek to quench their thirst. They were just finishing when they heard sharp popping sounds in the distance. Tembu George's head came up as he listened.

"Gunshots!" he said. "Come! Let us see if that is our quarry!" and he led his men away from the creek at a brisk pace. They had not gone far before they could hear yells as well as the shooting.

"I think we have a battle ahead of us," panted Tembu George. "I am guessing just beyond that ridge," he added, pointing with the heavy rifle he had removed from his shoulder.

They moved up the slope carefully and in a long parallel line so they would all appear at the crest simultaneously. They were not unaware of the effect the sudden appearance of a large group warriors would have on the opposition. Tembu George was in the middle with five Masai fighting men on each side of him. They were spaced about fifteen to twenty feet apart.

The M'Balla war chief and his warriors were unnoticed when they first topped the ridge as the fight going on below them had both sides completely occupied.

"It appears the slavers have stumbled upon a small safari," said Tembu George. "They left a small force to engage the safari while the others continued onward."

"It would seem the safari was in a bad way before the slavers found them," said Muwari. "I see half a dozen bodies on the ground and it seems there are only four left to fight. They will give up soon or they will all perish!"

"Let us drive the slavers off," said Tembu George. "Then we can learn what the situation is from the surviving members of the safari."

The warriors began moving down the slope, tapping their shields with the lion spears they carried. While about half of the group carried bows and arrows on their backs, they much preferred to do their fighting with spears.

They were halfway down the hillside when the first of the slavers saw the approaching warriors. Quickly he pointed them out to his companions.

"Masai! Masai!" came the frantic cries of the slavers as soon as they saw the height of the approaching fighters. Rapidly they broke into a run, skirting the small remaining group from the safari.

"I'll give them something to run for!" said Tembu George as he raised the heavy elephant gun to his shoulder. With the first loud thundering boom, the retreating slavers discarded their weapons and broke into an all out sprint to get away from the dreaded Masai.

"We can't waste a lot of time here," said Tembu George, "but we must see what the situation is with the remaining men of the safari. Perhaps they can tell us something of the slaves held by the invaders."

"I was looking forward to taking on the slavers!" declared Muwari.

"That time will still come," said Tembu George. "We don't have our women back yet!"

There were only four safari men still standing and they prepared to fight as they saw the approaching Masai as another fighting force.

When Tembu George saw the lone white man raise his rifle to his shoulder, he stopped and raised his arm. His men halted their approach. They were still spread out in a skirmish line.

"We come in peace, my friend," Tembu George called out in Swahili. The white man did not seem to understand.

"Do you speak English?" the M'Balla chief called loudly.

"Yes, I do," came the reply.

"We come as friends," Tembu George replied. "We are following a group of slavers but perhaps we can help you for a short while. What is your name?"

"I am Manfred Wilhelm," the man replied. "You arrived just in the nick of time!"

"Hmm," said Tembu George. "That sounds like German, yet you are speaking English. You wouldn't happen to be an American, would you?"

"I am German, but I have learned to speak English as well as my native language."

"I am Tembu George," the big man said. "I was born in America but I am now the chief of the M'Balla Masai. The slavers have taken my wife and others. We are out to get them back! What happened here?"

"To begin with, I think we are lost. Some of our boys deserted as we were getting too far away from their homeland. At least, that is the way I understood it. So we were low in numbers. We had decided to stop here and try to come to a decision as to what we should do. I am here to do some big game hunting, but that seems to be a waste of time now."

While Tembu George was talking with Manfred Wilhelm, Muwari stood listening as he partially understood English. The remaining Masai were checking over the dead and the wounded. They found three men still alive and were soon getting them cleaned up and their injuries properly treated. One of the remaining uninjured men from the safari was helping them and furnishing medical supplies and disinfectant to forestall infection.

Muwari, speaking softly in the Bantu dialect, said to his chief, "I see nothing here that would indicate he is hunting big game. There must be another reason for him being in this part of the country."

Tembu George nodded in agreement.

"Manfred Wilhelm," said George, "I assume you were not going to camp right here? There is no water and no protection."

"I don't know," replied the German. "My head boy was one of the casualties and he made the decisions. While I have been to Africa before this trip, I am not versed in handling a safari."

"We will move you with us," said Tembu George. "When we find water, if the location is suitable, we will set you up in camp. Your injured men need rest and some time to recuperate, but we will not be able to stay with you."

"We appreciate any help you can give us," said Manfred Wilhelm.

The lean tall Masai warriors soon had two stretchers fixed up for the safari men who had the worst injuries. The third was supported by his companions and the group moved out, following the trail of the slavers. Several of the Masai picked up the remaining safari equipment and carried it along with them.

"Mr. Wilhelm," said Tembu George as they walked, "I am an American, so perhaps you can forgive me if I seem somewhat confused. I was born and educated in Ohio. Later I came to Africa and am now, as I mentioned earlier, the chief of the M'Balla Masai."

"Oh," said Manfred Wilhelm, "where did you get your education?"

"You are thinking of colleges or universities where they hand out degrees and diplomas," replied George with a chuckle. "I was referring more to the school of hard knocks, although I do have some formal education."

"I don't quite understand," replied the German.

"It does not matter," replied Tembu George. "What I was leading up to, was to mention that your safari does not have the earmarks of a big game hunter's safari. In the eyes of myself and my warriors, you are here for another reason. Would you care to elaborate?"

Manfred Wilhelm looked surprised. Then slowly he shook his head. "When we get to camp and settled down, we will talk," he said.

"We are on the trail of slavers who took my wife and others from my tribe," said Tembu George firmly. "We do not have time to sit around and talk! We are traveling now at a walk! We should be running, but we are trying to help you out! You don't have to tell us anything! We can leave you right here and go after those slavers at a much faster pace! Or you can tell me now what you are doing in this part of the country! The choice is yours."

"I will tell you," replied the white man. "I just wanted some time to gather my thoughts."

"If you tell the truth," said the Masai leader, "you will not need to gather your thoughts!"

"I suppose you are right," the man replied. "I am in the military. Without knowing what was happening, I was suddenly thrust into this project. I am to search this part of the country in an effort to find wealth that is purported to be in the area. Wealth the Nazi party needs to carry on with their plans."

"Wealth in what form?" asked Tembu George.

"As silly as it seems," replied the German, "it is lost treasure. I believe it is precious metals and jewels that were placed in tombs with deceased kings and queens. However, we have questioned many natives and no one seems to have heard of any such thing in this region."

"Of course they haven't," replied George with a chuckle. "They don't want you looting the tombs of their ancestors. They may be natives and their culture may be different than yours, but that doesn't mean they are stupid. They are not going to tell you!"

"Oh," replied Wilhelm, disappointment in his voice. "I suppose you are right. Have you heard of such a treasure?"

"If I had, do you think I would tell you?" asked the big man walking beside the German.

"I suppose not," the white man agreed.

"What kind of information were you given before you left Germany? Were you given a specific location? Was there any name attached to the treasure you are attempting to find?"

"Just in this area somewhere," Manfred replied. "It seems there was an article in a newspaper, reprinted from a French paper, I believe. It claimed some British fellow who owns a large estate out here somewhere had found a vast amount of treasure on his holdings. Mostly gold bars, according to the story."

"Could it have been Irish? Or Scottish ?" asked Tembu George.

"Well, the article said British, but it could have been someone from Scotland or Ireland," the German said.

"Or Wales. Did the article give a name to either the Britisher or the location where he made his discovery?"

The man shook his head. "It seemed they didn't want to cause problems by identifying the fellow. But they claimed the treasure was comparable to Ophire or Opur or something like that. I think they were just grasping at straws. You ever hear of either one of those places or anything that sounded like that?"

"Just legend," replied Tembu George.

Muwari trotted up beside his chief, his arm outstretched as he pointed. "There is water over there," he said. "Perhaps a good place to set up the white man's camp."

"Lead the way," replied Tembu George.

It was dusk when the Masai left the camp of Manfred Wilhelm. They followed the trail of the slavers at a brisk run. For two hours they ran steadily and darkness had fallen when Tembu George called a halt.

"We are close," he said to his followers. "I want us to be rested before we encounter the slavers as they have gained in numbers. It may be more difficult to get our people back!"

"How long?" asked Muwari.

"Rest until a couple of hours after midnight," was the reply. "Then we will try to move up close where we can see what we are facing."

Heidi Wilhelm sat quietly on the small plane that droned southward from Berlin. She would land in Rome, make a switch and be back in the sky almost immediately. They would touch down in Tripoli and then head southeast. That was all she knew other than she would spend the night in some small out of the way airport in Africa.

Although the cabin of the plane was not chilly, the young woman gave an involuntary shiver. She pulled her jacket more tightly about her and her mind wandered. It had been a month since she had seen her husband, Manfred, and she wondered, with the political climate as it was, if she would ever see him again. She hoped so, for things had changed.

She thought back to that time when they had their last supper together, although neither had known it at the time. He had talked about a missing newspaper and at that point she wondered just how much he had deciphered about the situation as he really was not any dummy. And she had told him that she might be making another trip for her boss, something that she did fairly often. He had been so good about not prying into her job and just what she did with the distribution company for which she worked.

A tight lipped grim smile came to the young woman's face when she recalled her husband's comment about how nice it was that her employment was not tied in with the Nazi party or the military. If he had only known!

Heidi recalled when her supervisor came to her and said there was a young officer that his superiors wanted checked out and that she would be the perfect person to do so. Being loyal to her company and her country, she had agreed. She was instructed to get close to the young fellow, one Manfred Wilhelm, and when the time came she would be told what to ask in an effort to learn just what it was they wanted to know. Young Wilhelm turned out to be a very nice young man and as the months passed, he began to talk about a life together. At first Heidi was flustered and did not know how to respond. She liked the young man, but agreeing to marry him was not what she had started out to do. If she broke off her relationship with Manfred, she would feel terrible, but she didn't think she was in a situation where she could actually think of becoming his wife.

In frustration, she went to her supervisor and told him what was happening and that she did not know what she should do.

"Do you love this young man?" her boss had asked.

"I don't know," she had replied. "I probably could, given the right opportunity. I think I am a good actress and have caused him to fall for me. I am wondering if I should back off and, perhaps, be replaced by someone else."

"Hmmm," replied her supervisor, appearing to be in deep thought. "If we were to replace you, it would take months for a new girl friend to reach the point where you are presently. That is time we do not want wasted."

"I am unsure that I have actually been of any help in this project," Heidi had replied. Then her boss made the comment that stunned her.

"You have been excellent help," he replied. "And in an effort not to lose what you have gained for the party, I would suggest you accept this young man's proposal. Just keep in mind that you are married first to the Nazi party and this young officer comes second. Can you do that?"

Heidi had stood uncertainly, not knowing what to say. Her mouth had dropped open and she stammered twice before taking a deep breath and turning to look out the window as she got herself under control.

"Yes," she had whispered, "I can do that. I am shocked that it has come to this, but I can do it!" Then she reached out with her right arm and said in a sharp tone of voice, "Heil Hitler!"

Her boss had returned the salute.

Heidi had left her supervisor and that evening she told Manfred that she would be proud to be his wife.

Although, at her party's instructions, she had dragged her feet about actually setting a time for the marriage. Eventually, Manfred Wilhelm made the comment that it did not seem like she was going to marry him and that perhaps they should look elsewhere, see other people, and move on with their lives.

When Heidi reported this conversation to her supervisor, the man just smiled and said, "Then marry him! Don't keep the young man waiting!"

"The party is still keeping tabs on Manfred?" she had asked. "From all I have seen and heard, the man is everything the party could ask for. He is loyal and dedicated. He works hard..."

Her supervisor had held up his hand. "There are other things," he had said softly.

"Then perhaps I shouldn't..."

Again she was interrupted. "Your party has suggested you marry him," the man had said, almost sharply. "I would suggest you not waste anymore time. After all," he added, a leering touch to his voice, "it might be fun, you know!"

Heidi had colored prettily, saluted and left.

Within the week, Heidi and Manfred had married. The young woman had ceased to turn in reports concerning her husband.

A month after the wedding, this fact was brought to Heidi's attention. "You need to keep up a semblance of still keeping tabs on a person of interest," her boss had said.

"Why?" she had asked, somewhat pensively.

"Yours is not to question 'why," he had said, "but to follow orders! Do you understand?"

Heidi nodded mutely and gave the mandatory salute.

The young woman resumed turning in her weekly reports and the months flew by. Then Manfred had been interested in the newspaper article and had made comments about wishing to retire or perhaps work in civilian industry.

None of this appeared in Heidi's report and she was immediately sent out on another mission, something that only happened occasionally since she had married, much to her delight. She was completely unaware that their apartment had been bugged and that many of their conversations had been overheard.

When she returned from her assignment, looking forward to spending time with her husband, she found that the apartment was empty and she had the feeling it had been empty for some time. She became frantic and began searching the place, not knowing what she was looking for until she found it. A chill went through her body.

Quietly, she searched the rest of the apartment and found two more listening devices; one in the kitchen and one in the bedroom. She clenched her fists and blushed when she found the latter.

The following day she received another assignment and with this one, she began to ask herself why was this situation important in anyone? The answer that came to her mind was that they were keeping her busy and away from home.

She also realized that she was quite worried about Manfred and what had happened to him. She hoped that he was just out on some type of mission similar to what she was doing, but deep down inside, she was afraid this was not the case.

Heidi came to the conclusion that her husband was much more important to her than the party was. She knew how they thought. With the recent developments, she was sure someone wanted Manfred Wilhelm out of the way for some reason. She had been assigned to see that his downfall would come about. She was also sure that she was expendable, now that she had married the man.

Heidi Wilhelm looked out the window of the small twin engine plane. If she had been an emotional person, she would have shed tears. Instead, she sat silent, thinking.

This assignment in Africa, it was unlike anything she had ever been asked to do previously. In fact, she had been given very little information. She was just told that she would receive instructions when she reached her destination. This was not all that unusual.

However, there were some things that did not fit the usual assignment. First, they had dyed her blond hair a deep dark brown. She had been told some time back to begin growing the hair to a longer length, so it was now longer and fixed in a totally different style. She had been given two nose plugs that, when inserted properly, broadened her nose considerably. And finally she was given a small piece to put in her mouth that changed her voice. She was told to have it in place anytime she was around people and it definitely did change her voice.

They touched down in Italy, made the plane change and were in the air again with very little wasted time. She wasn't sure just where they went when they lifted off from an airport in Tripoli, but she knew the destination was somewhere in southeast Africa, above the equator.

It was dark when the small plane landed. Heidi was taken to small room that had several bunks located next to the area where oil and gasoline was stored. The smell was strong, but she was told to get as much rest as she could as they would be leaving before daylight.

It took a while, but she finally went to sleep. When she was aroused for the morning flight, she had a very strong headache from the gas fumes. She was handed a paper bag which contained a little food, but the throbbing head caused her not to eat any of it.

From the looks of the stars, she was sure they were continuing to fly in a southeasterly direction. She wondered what lay in that particular area that was of interest to the Nazi party.

Heidi Wilhelm dozed. She awoke when the plane made a bumpy landing. She picked up her valise and walked down the steps to the ground. The pilot brought her larger suitcase around and set it beside her.

"Where do I go?" she asked.

The man looked at her, frowned, shrugged his shoulders and walked away, moving toward what appeared to be a small hangar. Beyond that building and some distance away, were other structures, perhaps a settlement of sorts.

"I wonder if he even understood me?" she said to herself.

Then she heard the sound of a motor and in a moment an old flatbed truck appeared. The woman was somewhat surprised to see an actual motorized vehicle.

The truck came to a stop and the driver stepped out.

"You are Wilhelm?" he asked brusquely.

Heidi nodded without speaking. The man placed her large suitcase on the back of the truck and nodded for her to get in the cab. She did so.

They followed a poorly constructed dirt road for about ten minutes and then the driver turned the truck off the track and into the dark vegetation that had lined the route since they had left the airstrip. They stopped at the edge of a clearing where there were sixteen native bearers that the girl counted. There were also three men dressed in light European clothing and boots. She assumed this was the garb for the trek into the jungle.

Although she had a vague idea what all this was leading up to, she was anxious to hear just exactly what her assignment might be.

The three men were not black Africans, but they were exceedingly dark hued. She thought they might be Moroccans, as the shorter of the three was wearing a dusty red Fez. He was also quite stocky and seemed to be the leader.

"Welcome, Miz Wilhelm," he said in broken English. "Please excuse me for not speaking *Deutsch* as I do not understand it."

Heidi smiled. "Then we will speak English, if that is what you prefer."

"I am Ahmad," he said with a slight bow. "These two gentlemen are Hassan and Ismail. We are in charge of the safari and we shall be getting underway shortly. We were just waiting for your arrival. I trust your flight was agreeable?"

"I believe so," she said. "At least as much as one could expect."

Ahmad gave a wide toothy grin and nodded. He turned and issued several orders that Heidi did not understand. Then he turned back.

"I trust you can handle firearms?" he asked.

"Yes, I have been trained in shooting," Heidi replied.

"Hunya," the dark fellow called to a nearby native. Then he gave instructions that again the young woman did not understand. "Miz Wilhelm," he said, turning back to the girl. "Hunya will be your personal servant. He will bring you a rifle, pistol and ammunition. Keep it with you at all times. Hunya will be responsible for your valise and suitcase, although you may see other porters carrying it."

Heidi nodded.

Ahmad gave instructions to Hunya and the man immediately went to a supply box. In a few short moments, he returned carrying weapons. First, he handed Heidi a holstered pistol and ammunition belt.

The girl whispered "Thank you," and proceeded to belt the weapon about her waist. Then he handed her a rifle which she took.

"Why, this is a Lee-Enfield .303," she said with enthusiasm upon seeing the weapon was not of German make and therefore not likely to tie her to the Nazi cause. She began handling the weapon with familiarity until she

"I am Ahmad," he said…

realized Ahmad, Hassan and Ismail were all staring at her in surprise. At that point, Heidi decided the three fellows did not need to know how familiar she was with guns and other weapons.

Ahmad shouted several commands and the porters began picking up various bundles and boxes. Heidi was somewhat surprised at how much each man carried. Some of them had the load fixed in a pack they could carry on their backs while others hoisted the large bundles onto their heads and carried them in that manner.

Hunya picked up Heidi's gear and when he reached for her rifle, she stepped back and said "No!" in a stern voice. The man was slightly startled, but nodded that he understood.

All the blacks carried guns along with their loads. However there were six of the men who did not carry any supplies. They were heavily armed, both with rifles and pistols. They also carried their native weapons which included a belt knife and spear. Several even carried a bow with a quiver of arrows.

One of the armed natives led the way as the safari moved out, going in a southerly direction. He was followed by the three fellows in European dress. Then came three of the armed men with the remaining two heavily armed blacks being near the rear of the column. Ahmad and Hassan walked side by side directly behind the leader. Heidi had moved in next and soon found herself walking beside the man introduced as Ismail.

Heidi Wilhelm was a very physically fit person and she had little difficulty keeping up with the pace of the safari. The porters had not gone far when they began chanting as they walked.

"Why do they do that?" asked Heidi, looking at Ismail. "I thought it was prudent to be quiet when you were in the jungle."

"The boys chant when they are on the march because it makes the work easier. When we leave the area considered their homeland, they will not do the chanting."

Heidi smiled and nodded.

"Ismail," the woman said a short time later. "I was sent here from Berlin, however I have not been told what the purpose is. Do you know? Why are we out here?"

Ismail frowned and shook his head. "Not tell me," he finally grunted.

Heidi saw both Ahmad and Hassan look back when she asked the question. Since she had spoken in a normal tone of voice, she knew they were listening to what she was saying. And she had a feeling the three men knew the purpose of their journey, but did not feel they wanted to share that knowledge with her. Or, perhaps, they had been told to keep her in the dark.

Heidi Wilhelm felt like they had made good time that first day. There had been a few rest stops and in camp that evening, they had put up a small tent that was for her use. It was small but it would give her a modicum of privacy.

The second day the safari moved quietly without the chanting and the young woman found that she actually missed the jovial sound of the bearers. The terrain was a little more rugged and in places the vegetation was thick enough to require the use of machetes to hack their way through. The jungle itself seemed to be dark and mysterious.

"Just where are we going?" asked Heidi that evening as they ate food prepared by the natives. "It seems to me we are making good time. But how long before we will reach our destination?"

Ahmad smiled and stretched his short legs out in front of him as he sat on a log pulled near the fire by the porters. Hassan sat on the log as well. Ismail and Heidi both sat cross-legged on the ground.

"I believe we are far enough into our journey that we can share our destination with you," said Ahmad. "We have been hired to find the location of Offur and the treasure that is rumored to be there. It is difficult to determine just where this place is located. There are many stories, but you have to know the right people before you can hear them."

Ahmad hesitated for a moment and Hassan spoke up. "There are many stories and there are at least as many different names for the place. That, perhaps, is why it has been so difficult to determine a location. If it were easy to find, the treasure would already have been looted."

"How close are we to where ever it is that you are taking us?" the woman asked.

Ahmad shrugged. "Two more days, maybe three, will put us somewhere in the area. We do not know exactly where it is that we are going. Once there, we will have to do a lot of scouting about the territory."

"Who are you working for?"

"Your superiors," said Ahmad softly. "We are to find this vast treasure and you are to determine just what your government can use. Then we can help ourselves to the remainder," he added with his toothy grin. "We make sure you get back to the air strip. Then it is up to you to get the wealth back to your superiors."

Heidi's mind was whirling. All along, she was under the impression her husband had secretively been sent to Africa for this very reason. If she were sent for this treasure, then where was Manfred? What had happened to him?

Her concern for her husband made it very clear to Heidi Wilhelm that she now considered Manfred much more important to her than the Nazi party for which she worked. She was beginning to understand that someone, for some reason, wanted Manfred Wilhelm out of the way. Their first step was an effort to find something they could use against him. With that thought in mind, they had procured the services of Heidi Wilhelm. When that failed to give them the information they wanted, they had bugged the apartment. When she had married Manfred that made her a liability as well.

Heidi was an intelligent girl. She worried most of that night and obtained very little sleep. She did come to the conclusion that her husband had very likely been sent to Africa under the pretenses of looking for the hidden treasure. It would be simple enough to do away with him on some safari without anyone being the wiser. If that were the case, then why was she here? Evidently they, whoever *they* were, wanted her out of the way, too. Was this safari an elaborate attempt to dispose of her? She decided it was and that she should be very careful.

The following three days were harder as the jungle was thicker and there were no easy trails to follow. However, since the talk around the evening fire, the three men seemed more at ease around Heidi and would visit with her when she asked questions.

Her servant, Hunya, took it upon himself to teach the girl to speak Swahili and was continually pointing at various things and saying the name. He had started on the first day and after the fifth day; Heidi was beginning to grasp enough of the language that she would slowly say sentences and ask questions, much to the delight of all the blacks.

It was on the fifth evening when they were again around a supper fire, that Heidi asked if they were in the vicinity of the fabled treasure.

"Let me check with Bunto," said Ahmad, referring to the native who was leading them. "We should be getting close." He got up and walked over to the fire where the blacks were eating.

Thinking of something, Heidi got up and walked to her tent and in so doing passed relatively close to Ahmad and Bunto. She wasn't trying to listen in on their conversation, but she couldn't help hearing part of it. For a moment, she stopped cold. Then, shaking uncontrollably, she went on to her tent.

She had distinctly heard Ahmad say to Bunto that tomorrow they would get rid of the white woman and then look for the treasure themselves. Both men had broken into laughter.

Heidi picked up her nail file and returned to the campfire and the remainder of her evening meal, although she had lost all appetite for eating it.

"Bunto thinks we should be in the vicinity of the legendary treasure by sometime tomorrow," said Ahmad as he returned and settled down by the fire.

Heidi nodded, not daring to speak as she was sure her voice would break. She coughed and forced herself to finish the meal. When she was finished, she stood up stretched and yawned. Having left the impression she was tired, she returned to her tent.

She reasoned that she had until the following day to find a moment when she could slip away. Perhaps sometime tonight when all the rest of the camp was asleep. As she thought of, and discarded, various plans, she was aware that in the five days they had traveled, not once had they seen a dangerous beast or a native from another tribe. Surely she could back track to the air strip.

Heidi came to the conclusion that as soon as the camp had settled down for the night, she would slip out and try to follow their back trail. If she could get a few hours head start, she might be able to evade the pursuit that was sure to follow.

Previously, she had not paid much attention to the night guards stationed around the camp, but she did so now. She also fixed up her small valise with what essentials she thought she would have to have to survive. Everything else she would leave behind. She checked her pistol and rifle and waited.

The young woman was sure it was past midnight when she slipped out of her tent. She had a small pack on her back, the pistol around her waist and she carried the Lee-Enfield ready to use at a second's notice. She had picked out the two sentries' locations and avoided going anywhere near them. She also felt that should they see her, they would assume she was answering a call of nature and ignore her.

Once in the sheltering darkness of the jungle, Heidi picked up the path they had made in approaching their campsite. She followed it as quickly as she could, trying to keep any noise down until she was a sufficient distance from the sleeping safari. Once away from the camp, she ran hard for a quarter of a mile and then stopped to catch her breath.

Heidi was panting, breathing deeply, when she heard the noise and her blood ran cold. They had evidently discovered her absence as there was much yelling and then she was hearing gunshots. With that, a wave of relief swept over her.

The camp had been attacked just after she had slipped away! With any luck, they would assume she was either killed or taken prisoner by the attackers. The sound of gunshots, war cries and men screaming and yelling lent wings to the young woman's feet.

Heidi did not know how long she had traveled, but it seemed like she had been going all night. She found a large tree near the trail she was backtracking and climbed into the lower branches to rest. She was soon sound asleep.

Tembu George and his Masai settled down to rest for a short while before moving up on the slavers' campsite, which they were sure was not too far along the trail. The warriors stretched out on the ground, chewing dried meat as they rested.

They had not been resting for many minutes before Tembu George stood up. Muwari saw him get to his feet and stood up as well.

"You intend to go on?" asked the sub chief.

"I cannot wait," said George. "To be here resting when our women are held as slaves not far away... it just eats at me! I shall go ahead and locate the camp. Then I shall watch and see what is taking place. When the men are rested, you bring them up and we will decide what action to take at that time."

Muwari smiled and nodded as Tembu George turned and disappeared into the semi darkness following the obvious trail left by the fleeing slavers. Not only could the big man see the trail, but he could also catch the scent of his quarry.

Tembu George expected to travel at least a couple of miles before finding the camp, but he was pleasantly surprised when after covering approximately half a mile, he caught the strong odor of woodsmoke. He also began to hear slight sounds coming from the activity within the slavers camp.

The Masai chieftain approached the camp silently and then climbed a huge tree knowing that the slavers would expect any enemy to approach at ground level and, therefore, did not spend much time looking upward in the trees.

The group that had taken Othoya, Shaliba and her sisters was small, numbering six total. They had been joined by nine others earlier in the day, making a total of fifteen men. The slavers had been in a skirmish with the Wilhelm safari a few hours earlier, but they had suffered nothing more than minor wounds while inflicting heavy losses on the safari. Much of that was due to the Wilhelm safari being poorly organized and under equally poor leadership.

As Tembu George stretched out on the huge limb where he could observe the camp, one of the first things he did was count the number of men. He came up with fifteen, the number he thought would be there. Othoya was wearing a slave collar and his hands were manacled behind his back. He had been placed near the fire and looked very dejected.

What bothered Tembu George was that he did not see any of the three women around the slavers campsite. Finally, the Masai chief silently went back to the ground and circled the entire area looking for a place where the women might be held. He found nothing. Yet he was sure they were still with the group earlier in the day.

Meanwhile, the resting Masai realized their chief had gone ahead without them. It was not long before they had convinced Muwari that they were rested and should be joining Tembu George. The sub chief agreed and the ten warriors were soon following the spoor left by the slavers.

The Masai were equally surprised at how quickly they came upon the camp. They faded into the jungle darkness and Muwari gave the chattering cry of a monkey. To their surprise, a reply came from a spot less than fifty yards away.

"They have fifteen men in camp," said Tembu George in a low voice. "Othoya is bound by the fire, but I have been unable to locate Shaliba or her sisters. That means I shall need to talk to their leader as I must know what happened to the women."

"Let us wait until someone leaves the camp," said Muwari. "Then we will take him and go far enough away that he cannot call out for help. Then we will find out where the women are being held!"

Tembu George and his men had just taken their positions when one of the slavers left the campsite on the opposite side. It appeared that he was going after more wood for the fire.

Like wraiths of the night, the Masai circled the area and came upon the fellow gathering wood from a dead tree. He was making enough noise as he broke the limbs that he did not hear the silent approaching warriors.

A large hand clamped around the fellow's throat and another went over his mouth. He reached to pull at the stifling hands but others grabbed his arms and pulled them out straight. Then he felt his legs grasped and he was carried away, unable to struggle or resist in any manner.

The Masai carried the fellow a good distance from the camp and then placed him flat on the ground but still held tightly. Tembu George released his grip slightly on the throat and mouth.

"Do you understand me?" George asked in Swahili.

The man nodded his head.

"Good," replied Tembu George. "I am going to release your mouth and if you cry out, I shall slit your throat from ear to ear! Do you understand me?"

Again the man nodded.

"Where are the women you took as slaves?"

"They were sold," the fellow stammered.

"Sold!" exclaimed the chief. "How so? They were with you late this afternoon!"

"Putai, our leader, met with some men while we were fighting with a small safari. They wanted the women and he sold them. That is all I know."

"Where were they going?" asked Tembu George harshly.

"I do not know," the man said, quivering. "Only Putai could tell you. Even he might not know as those who deal in slaves do not like to let others know where they can be found."

Tembu George nodded. "Is there any way to get Putai out of the camp?"

The man shook his head. "He is very lazy."

Tembu George rose to his feet. "There are four men standing as guards around the camp," he said to his Masai. "I want them rendered unconscious. Slip up and whack them with the butt of your spears. When I see that all four are sleeping, I will walk into the camp with our friend here and talk to this Putai. I want the ten of you to circle the camp so that when I tell the slaver to look around, he will see all of you and it will give the impression of being the front edge of a large group."

The Masai smiled at their leader. The time for action was drawing near.

"When do we begin to take them down?" asked Muwari.

"Just as soon as something goes wrong," replied Tembu George. "I would like to find out where our women have been taken before we start killing them! But if they are stubborn, perhaps a few dead bodies can change their mind. Let's go!"

Tembu George stood beside the man who had gone to fetch wood. One hand covered the fellow's mouth and the other held a sharp knife touching his throat.

"Be very careful," whispered the chief. "You could come out of this alive, if you do exactly as you are told."

The man gave an imperceptible nod, being very careful of the keen blade pressed against his throat.

As they watched, Tembu George saw each of the guards slump as though they had gone to sleep. Only once did he actually see the butt of a spear whack the guard across his skull. The Masai were working in pairs with one warrior knocking the guard out while the other caught him from behind and lowered him gently to the ground.

"Do you know what this is?" asked Tembu George, holding his pistol in front to the man.

"Yes, it is a gun."

"I am putting my knife back in my belt," said the chief. "If you try to run or make any warning sound, I will just shoot you dead and my warriors will slaughter your camp before they know what has hit them! Do you understand?"

Again, the man nodded.

With his hand on the back of the man's neck, Tembu George entered the slavers' camp.

"Lead me directly to Putai," he whispered harshly.

There were several men busy around the fire and one man was seated on a stone close to the flickering blaze. He did look very smug and Tembu George frowned. He did not appear to be someone who would listen to reason.

"Maug!" exclaimed a man at the fire. "Where is the wood?" Then his mouth dropped open as he saw the big man right behind Maug.

The man on the stone realized something was wrong and leaped to his feet.

"Putai," said Tembu George in a deep booming voice. "I am the chief of the Masai! I am Tembu George and I am here to talk with you!"

The slaver was obviously shaken and began to look around frantically. That was when he realized his camp was surrounded by the tall fierce Masai.

"Earlier today," said George, "you sold three women. I want to know who you sold them to and where they were taken."

Immediately Putai sensed that he had something the big Masai wanted. Now he could bargain. "Let us sit and talk," said Putai with an ill concealed smirk.

Tembu George reached out and grasped the smaller man by the shirt, lifting him off the ground. "I want to know where my women are and I want to know right now!" he thundered.

Putai started to make some kind of reply when a shot rang out and

Tembu George felt the burn of a bullet across his shoulder.

Instinctively, he flipped Putai away from him and recoiled backwards. Unfortunately Tembu George was facing the cooking fire and while the flames had burned down, the coals were still red hot. The war cries of the Masai were ringing through the night air as Putai landed on his backside right in the center of the fire.

The howling squall of terror was equal to any war cry the Masai were shouting. Putai thrust his hands down, pushing himself upwards and out of the burning embers. Both hands were burned and the seat of his loosely fitting pantaloons were blazing. The fellow was screeching in pain as he rushed by Tembu George. The big Masai chief reached out, grabbed the fellow and threw him on the ground.

There was another shot fired and Tembu George stopped to see who was doing the shooting. When he located the shooter, he simply pulled his revolver and shot the slaver on the opposite side of the clearing.

Putai had leaped to his feet and was starting to run again, still howling, when Tembu George reached out and thrust him to the ground once more. This time he dropped beside the shrieking fellow and began rolling him in the dirt. In moments the fire was out.

The slave leader was still squawking incoherently. Tembu George clouted him a stunning blow across the face. The fellow stopped and looked bewildered.

"Get the keys and free that man you have shackled by the fire!" snapped the Masai chief.

Putai looked as though he did not know what Tembu George had asked.

"You get that man out of his chains," barked the Masai leader, "or I will stick your back side in the fire again!"

Putai had his keys out and was unlocking the manacles and neck collar immediately. The Masai brought over five more of the slavers. With Putai and the four unconscious guards, that made ten survivors out of the fifteen.

Tembu George moved over beside Putai. "Where did the people who bought our women go?" he asked.

"I do not know," the leader said. "They do not tell us such things!"

"You've been in this business a long time," said Tembu George. "Where do you think they went? What kind of men were they?"

Putai acted as though he were thinking.

"Muwari," said Tembu George, "while Putai is considering his options, I want you and the our warriors to gather every weapon you can find and put them on the fire. Not the firearms, of course, as they could go off and injure someone. When that is done and we still do not have an answer from our friend here, begin stripping the clothes from them and add them to the fire. When there is nothing else to burn, we will start roasting slavers!"

"They were horsemen from the north," said one of the slavers. "They rode back to the north when they left here. They will be far away by now."

"You have three mules," said Tembu George. "We will take those as they will help some. And Muwari, search the slavers for the money they received in payment for our women! That belongs to the women and to Othoya. Incidentally," said Tembu George, turning to the just freed slave, "choose what weapons you would like before the warriors have burned them. Take as much as you want. You will travel with us and we will likely be in another battle soon."

When Tembu George and the Masai left the camp of the slavers, it was in shambles. There was not a weapon to be found and most of the clothing had been burned. Only enough cloth was left for loin cloths. There had been coins on three of the slavers. The money was placed in a small pouch and hung on a saddle.

Just as they were ready to move out, Othoya asked Tembu George if he had the key to the shackles and the big man handed it to him. The former slave went to the fire and picked up the discarded neck ring and manacles. He walked over to Putai and fastened the ring around his neck and locked it. Then he placed the metal bracelets on the slaver's burned wrists and snapped them into place.

"Perhaps," he said, "by the time you have arrived home, they will have rusted enough that you can break out of them. I'm taking the key with me!"

The Masai placed Othoya on one of the mules and gave him lead ropes for the remaining two animals. Then they hit a steady lope following the trail of the group that had bought their women from Putai.

It was an hour before dawn when they came upon a clearing where some type of skirmish had taken place. There were numerous bodies strewn about the area and there were three horses grazing.

"It would appear to me the slavers were wiped out," muttered Tembu George. "Search carefully and make sure the bodies of our women are not among the dead."

In a short time, they were convinced their women had been taken with the new group. And it seemed the attackers or ambushers had been a native people of some kind and that they had numbered several times more than the slavers. They soon found the trail leading away to the west.

"I think," said Tembu George, "this battle may have been going on about the same time as our little skirmish with Putai and his fellows."

Muwari nodded in agreement adding, "It appears many of them were shot with arrows. Many of the wounds were not enough to cause death, but there they are."

"My guess would be there was poison on the arrows," said Tembu George. "We must be aware of that when we approach them."

At first the Masai were reluctant to ride the horses and mules, but when Tembu George pointed out how much more rested they would be by riding instead of running, they began to take turns riding. By dawn they were pushing along the trail rather rapidly and with the direction they were going, they soon entered a thicker, darker jungle where the light always seemed to be gloomy.

Heidi Wilhelm awoke in the early morning light to the sound of men running and the occasional word being uttered. She wondered if they were the safari members and if they had come to the decision that she had deserted them. She was in a gloomy dark spot in the crotch of the tree, but she could see the trail.

The natives coming back over the trail were, indeed, the men from her safari. At first she wanted to call out to them, but knowing they were most likely all in on the plan to get rid of her, she decided she was better off on her own.

The men on the trail looked very angry and she noticed that most of them had wounds of some sort. Some were still bleeding. Then it hit her; there were only five of them! Out of the nineteen safari members, there were only five of them left and neither Hunya nor Bunto was with the group. She could understand their anger and she was also sure she wanted nothing more to do with them.

Heidi's first feeling was to get down from the tree and flee in the opposite direction. Then she realized she would be going directly toward the group that had attacked the camp after she had left. She did not want that. She decided to stay in the tree and see if any stragglers might come by, not that she would contact them but she did not want to run into them on the trail.

After an hour and nothing had happened, she gathered up her weapons which she had spent the time cleaning, and clamored down the tree. She was about to step onto the trail left by the passage of her safari the previ-

She decided to...see if any stragglers might come by.

ous day, when she stopped. If someone should come along the trail and see her footprints, they might decide to follow her. She would be leaving boot prints which would indicate she was not native and since her foot would be somewhat smaller, a good tracker would probably deduce she was female.

Heidi decided she could go east as that was the side of the trail where the tree was in which she had spent the night. That way she wouldn't have to cross the trail. She had no idea which way would be the best to go, either east or west. She went east so she would not leave any tracks on the trail.

There was no trail to follow and she had no machete with which to cut away growth to let her pass easily. Soon she realized she was just wandering and she began to have a feeling of hopelessness. Not only that but she was both hungry and thirsty.

Eventually she found a stream of clear water and quenched her thirst. She was tired, thirsty and of the opinion that she should have tried to join the safari members when they passed near her tree earlier. She found a big tree and climbed into the branches to spend the night. She heard many sounds that night that she was unfamiliar with and decided they had probably been there in the jungle every night but she just hadn't been concerned about them.

The following day was more of the same. She did find some berries that she had seen the safari members eat as they moved along. She tried some and decided that, while they would not be her favorite, they were edible.

Finally in the late afternoon the young woman stopped and sat down at the base of a large tree. She would try to rest and do some thinking about what would be the best thing to do.

When she awoke, her could hear voices. Frightened, she got behind the tree and tried to listen. If they were speaking a language she understood, she would try to approach them.

Heidi heard a man laugh and it sounded like an easy going fellow. Stretched out on the ground, she tried to get in position to see what might be coming as she did believe the sounds were moving toward her. She placed the Lee-Enfield beside her, ready for action.

When the group came into the open, they looked something like a war party. There were three horses and three mules. About half the group was riding and about half were walking. They seemed to be quite tall and most of them carried large shields and huge spears.

Then she heard one of the men speaking say the word *George* and she almost leaped for joy as that was a word she understood.

She picked up her rifle and waited until they group was a little closer before she stepped out into the open.

Since George was an English name, she spoke English when she called out to them. The group stopped in surprise. Then a large man stepped around a horse and came forward to meet her.

"Who is it, out here in the jungle, who speaks English?" he asked pleasantly.

"I am Heidi and I am lost," she said quickly. "My safari was attacked and not many survived. Can you help me? Would you let me go with you?"

"I am Tembu George, chief of the M'Balla Masai," smiled the big man facing her. "We are on the trail of some slavers, but you are welcome to join us, if you wish. When our mission here is complete, we will take you back with us and help you get to civilization. Would that be acceptable?"

"Oh, my, yes!" Heidi exclaimed.

"You appear to be tired," said Tembu George. "I shall put you on one of the horses. I see you are carrying a pistol and a rifle. You might be of some help when we meet up with the slavers we are following."

Heidi smiled and nodded. She was grateful when one of the tall men handed her a small sack that had dried food in it.

"Food," he said in English.

"Oh, do you speak English, too?" she asked.

"He is learning," said Tembu George, with a smile.

"I was trying to learn Swahili," said Heidi, "before the attack."

"Perhaps we can continue to help you with that," the big chief said.

They had not traveled far and Heidi was beginning to enjoy the fact that she could ride and not have to do all that walking or running. She gazed about her as they moved along and she was thinking how beautiful and mysterious the jungle was. Then she noticed something huge swinging high up in one of the trees. It looked very much like some kind of nest and she pointed it out to Tembu George.

"What is it?" she asked.

"That is a trap," the man said. "It was a net placed on the ground. When something walked on it and triggered a string, the net wrapped around whatever it was that had sprung the trap. A bent over tree is released and jerks the whole thing up in the air. The animal is held until the hunter comes to check his trap."

"There is something in that net, isn't there?" Heidi asked.

"Yes, but we did not catch it," Tembu George replied. "We will leave it for the hunter that did."

At that point there came the faint sound of a human voice.

"That came from the net," said Muwari. "We should check and see who is caught."

"We can't just cut him down," said Tembu George. "The fall would likely kill him."

Quickly the Masai climbed the tree and fastened a rope to the top. Then by running the rope under a heavy lower branch of a nearby tree, they pulled the net low enough they could open it. As they worked to get the net opened without ruining it, they began to carry on a conversation in Swahili with the imprisoned fellow.

The captive was a little man standing near five feet in height and was brown in color, including the large amount of hair on his body. He was very grateful and indicated he had been in the trap for several hours

"What are you called?" asked Muwari.

"I am Moa of the Minginka," he said. "We came out of our valley to do some hunting, but we have had nothing but bad luck."

"Did you have a problem with some slavers several miles back?" asked Tembu George.

"We did," Moa replied. "Before dawn, they raided our camp. We did not know they were anywhere around. We ran into the jungle, regrouped and came back to surround them. We did not leave many. Only those who ran fast."

"Do you use poison on your arrows?" asked Tembu George.

"We do," Moa nodded, not bothering to justify the use.

"For many days we have been on the trail of the slavers as they took several of our young women," said Tembu George. "Since we did not find their bodies, we assume you took them with you when the battle was over."

"Ah, yes!" Moa exclaimed. "We removed their chains and took them with us. They seemed to be quite hungry. My father, Hun, is trying to decide what to do with them. We Minginka do not take slaves, so they are of little use to us. You come with me. I will take you to our camp and you can see the women."

"Let us go immediately," said Tembu George.

The war chief of the M'Balla Masai learned much about the Minginka as they strode along the trail of the people who now held his wife and her two sisters. In less than an hour they were nearing the camp.

"I think it best," said Moa, "that your warriors stop here. We do not want to start another battle and my people are very apprehensive now. I will explain to Hun how your men got me down from the tree trap. Then everyone should be happy!"

"Good," replied Tembu George, giving Muwari a slight nod before striding off with Moa toward the Minginka contingent.

The Masai chief walked beside the diminutive warrior as they approached the camp. He carried a rifle in one hand and in the other, held a Masai lion spear. About his waist was strapped a pistol and knife.

Tembu George reckoned there to be around forty of the Minginka warriors in the camp. He looked about and was immediately relieved to see Shaliba and her sisters not far away. He raised the hand holding the spear in greeting and they all waved in return, smiling at the big man.

"Father," said Moa as they approached a man showing gray in his hair, "this is Tembu George. He and his friends saved me from a trap in the jungle. I believe I owe my life to him."

Hun smiled. "Thank you for returning my son to me. We were simply waiting for his return before we set out for our valley. Would you like to accompany us?"

"Tembu George and his Masai have been following the slavers who took his wife and two other women from their tribe. They are the women we have with us. I believe we should return them to their people."

"I have been giving some thought to this," said Hun. "The Minginka have never had slaves and we have prided ourselves in that we did not need someone enslaved to take care of us. But I am wondering if the time has come for us to move forward and take a few slaves to make our lives more comfortable."

Tembu George stood tall before the Minginka leader. "The Masai share your belief that no man or woman should be a slave! The Masai are the most feared warriors in the jungle or on the veldt! We do not hold slaves and we drive away those who would come into our country in an effort to take slaves! Had the brave Minginka not wiped out the slavers that held my wife and her friends, my warriors would have!"

The Masai chief stopped to give the Minginka leader time to think about what he had said. When he paused, Moa spoke up.

"Father," he said, "had not the Masai stopped to free me from the trap; I would have been dead by sundown. It is my belief we should treat them as friends and return their women to them!"

"That also has merit," the old man said, nodding his head. "However, I see only a few warriors that follow this Masai chief. We could have a dozen fine slaves just for the taking."

"You do not understand our weapons," said Tembu George firmly. "We have the thunder sticks that strike from far away. Should you decide to take us as slaves, there will be a battle. And, my friend Hun, you will be the first to fall. Then what good will the slaves be for you?"

Hun frowned. "I do not think you have that capability," he finally said. "The slavers who held your women had boom sticks and they all fell."

"I believe you hid in the forest and shot them with poisoned arrows," replied Tembu George. And he realized as he said it, that he should not have. The man's face displayed his anger.

"Let us have a small demonstration," the Masai said quickly. "Bring three melons or gourds. Place them on sticks like a man's head. Then watch."

Hun continued to glare at Tembu George. Then he turned and said something in his own language to the men behind him. Immediately they began procuring sticks and gourds. The Masai Chief had them set the poles in the ground about thirty yards from where the Minginka leader sat. Then they placed the gourds, the approximate size of a man's head, on the top of the sticks which were about ten feet apart.

Tembu George walked back to Hun. "I want you to remember that the Masai do not believe in slavery," he said. "You do not want us as an enemy. You see up the slope a short distance the ten Masai warriors. They are close enough for the thunder sticks to strike anyone in this camp. When we enter a battle, the first thing we do is eliminate the leader or chief. If we were to go into battle right now, most of the effort would be to take down the leaders. You know who would be the first to die, my friend!"

Hun's face grew darker as he was not in the habit of being told what he could and could not do.

"First," said Tembu George, "I must signal to my warriors that this is only a demonstration because if they think I have been fired on, you know who the first casualty will be, my friend."

With that he turned and faced the slope where the small group of Masai stood waiting. He waved with a zig-zag motion over his head. He was sure they already knew what he was doing with the set up of gourds on sticks. He also knew that Heidi was the only one with a gun, but the Minginka did not know that.

Tembu George moved away from where Hun was sitting. That also opened up space for a clear shot from the Masai on the slope.

"Let us pretend," said Tembu George, "that you are the man in the middle. Your son is on one side and your military leader is on the opposite side. If you were to start a battle with us, this is what would happen."

Tembu George quickly raised the big elephant gun and in rapid succession fired three shots with a gourd exploding with each shot.

"At this point," said the Masai chief, turning to face Hun, "the battle is about ten seconds old! I will remind you that I am your friend until you prove me wrong."

Hun stood up, visibly shaken."Bring the women," he ordered. "We are late in returning to our valley," he said to Tembu George. "We are pleased to return the slaves to you."

"Thank you," said Tembu George. "Likewise, we are happy to have been of service to your son. Until we meet again," he added.

The three women appeared from behind a group of warriors and wisely kept their faces stoic as they were shoved towards George. They could sense the situation was still tense.

"Shaliba," he said softly in the M'Balla dialect, "go join Muwari quickly. I will be along in a moment."

The three women hurried up the slope while Tembu George smiled and waved at Hun and Moa. Once all the Minginka warriors had passed him and were moving with their leaders, he turned and made his way up the slope where Shaliba threw herself into his arms.

"We knew you would come," she whispered.

Tembu George placed the three women on the mules and horses, along with Othoya and Heidi. "Now," he said, "we are going to travel somewhat rapidly until we are so far away that a small group of Minginka cannot return and shoot poison arrows at us! Let's run!"

It was an hour and a half later that the group stopped for water and a short rest. They had covered a good distance and were near the site where the Minginka had slaughtered the slavers.

"When we arrive at the battle ground," said Tembu George to Muwari, "I want to you search those bodies that might be carrying coins."

"Why the sudden interest in coins?" asked the sub chief.

"We have a white woman with us who will need to return to civilization," Tembu George replied. "It is very likely she will need the money to return to her own people."

Muwari nodded. The Masai chief turned and walked over to where the woman was resting.

"Heidi," said Tembu George, "what is your last name? You did not tell us that."

"Yes," she said, "I wanted to make sure what your feelings were toward the Germans before I told you. My last name is Wilhelm."

"I wondered," said the Masai chief softly. "In a short time, we will have a surprise for you." And he smiled as everything was falling neatly into place.

The Masai pushed themselves and the horses and mules. Night fell and they stopped briefly. At this point, Tembu George called Muwari to one side.

"I have a feeling," he said, "that Hun may have sent some of his men after us with their poison arrows. At the rate we have been traveling, they have been unable to catch us. However, if they do, we will likely be unaware they are out there until one of our number falls dead from a poisoned arrow. I want you to take five men and the horses and mules. Move back along the trail a short distance and wait. If they show up, take care of them! They will have one purpose and that is to kill us. Get them first, but beware of their poison arrows. When you have taken care of them, ride the horses and mules and catch up with us. We are moving directly toward Manfred Wilhelm's camp."

Muwari picked the five men he wanted and they mounted the steeds. Tembu George stepped up beside the animal he was riding. "We will continue to rest here for a short time. Then we will resume our trek. I think by tomorrow morning we should be in the white man's camp."

The sub chief smiled and nodded. Then with a motion of his hand, he and his men rode back along the trail.

When Tembu George felt like his group had rested long enough, he got them on their feet and prepared to continue their journey.

"We will walk, not run," he said with a grin. "But we will walk rather rapidly. It is dark now, but presently there will be good moonlight. We will be able to see well enough."

The Masai chief raised his hand and listened intently. Then he turned to one of the warriors standing beside him.

"What do you hear?" he asked in a very low voice.

"I hear the sound of a battle," the man replied. "Our men have encountered the Minginka sooner than expected."

"You take this group and keep moving," said Tembu George. "I will hurry back to join Muwari and our fighters. The Minginka will be surprised what the gun can do!"

He raised his hand in a wave to his people and then he began running. He knew the fight taking place could not be too far away or they would not have been able to hear it.

When he arrived at the scene of the conflict, he found his Masai had taken shelter among several large boulders near the center of a rock strewn glade. He located the horses and mules not far away grazing.

Tembu George settled in behind a rock that was about waist high. It seemed there were about a dozen of the little brown men and they were staying well out of reach of the long spears of the Masai. He could see them hiding among the bushes and sending their poisoned arrows toward the warriors in the rocks.

Tembu George used the boulder where he crouched to steady in big gun. Then he methodically began firing at the poison people. His first three shots took out three men and splattered their remains over their comrades. He hesitated to see if they would flee but they did not. Systematically he began dropping the brown warriors. Shortly, he thought he saw three dark shadows disappear over the rise in the moonlight.

"I think they have left," he called to Muwari.

"Yes, they are gone," the sub chief replied. "You would have thought they could see what was happening and retreated earlier. We counted thirteen of them when they first jumped us. I think there are ten bodies out there now."

"You were going to wait until they had used up their poison arrows," commented Tembu George, "and then take them in hand-to-hand combat?"

"Yes," Muwari replied. "It would have taken a good deal longer, but the result would have been the same."

They did not bother with the bodies of their enemies. The Masai believed the human body poisoned the ground and the remains were left for the jungle to destroy.

It was after midnight when Tembu George and the Masai caught up with their friends.

"Let us move off the track we have been following," said the chief, "and rest for a while. Our group has to be very worn out. The horses and mules need to eat and rest as well."

"George," said Heidi, approaching the man and Shaliba, "you said there would be a surprise, but I have been unable to figure out what it could be. Is there any chance you could tell me?"

Tembu George laughed lightly. "If I tell you," he said, "I do not think you will be able to sleep."

"It is bad news, then, huh?"

"Oh, I wouldn't say that," smiled the big man. "Do you know a fellow named Manfred?"

"Manfred?" she asked. "Manfred? I was married to a Manfred once, but the party got rid of him! At least, that is what I think. No one would tell me anything and then I was sent on this expedition and it was primarily to make me disappear! I believe they wanted to get rid of both of us for some reason. But I haven't been able to figure out just why."

"A few days ago," said Tembu George, "we came across a fellow who said his name was Manfred. Most of his safari had either left him or been killed as slavers had attacked him. We put him and his surviving fellows in a camp not far from here with the promise we would pick him up on our way back through.

"Can you describe him?" asked Heidi quickly.

"Better than that," said the chief. "His last name was Wilhelm!"

Heidi gave a happy squeal. Then she reached into her mouth and removed a small item which she threw into the darkness.

"Oh, that feels better," she said and her voice was totally different in sound. "And I had nose plugs that changed the shape of my face somewhat," she added. "I got rid of those after our safari was attacked and before I met you guys. And my hair is grown out now and the coloring has been changed, so I hope Manfred will recognize me!"

"Just remember, Heidi," said Tembu George, "Manfred has been through a lot, too. And from what I've been hearing from you, I don't think you want to return to Germany. I'm sure your party thinks you are dead. So now is a good time to go to another part of the world, change your name somewhat and start over in a new life!"

"Oh, if we only could!" the young woman exclaimed.

"You are thinking of the expense of passage, right? We have gathered up a bag full of coins and other wealth from the slain slavers. We have no need for it, but I am sure you and Manfred could put it to good use!"

"Oh, thank you!" the girl exclaimed. "Tomorrow will be the first day of our new life! Thanks to you, Tembu George, and your Masai!"

THE END

N'GEESO AND THE SILVER BIRD

The blazing African sun had little mercy on anything below it. Heat waves shimmered across the tree tops, dancing in the spasmodic breeze. Birds and animals alike sought relief from the incessant heat.

N'Geeso, the four foot tall chief of the Kamazila Pygmy tribe, wondered why he was out in the intense heat but he was sure it was just the wanderlust in his heart. Surely it had nothing to do with a lapse of intelligence. However, he was the only member of his tribe out and about in the heat. The others had the good sense to stay out of the oven-like temperature.

The chief rubbed his little pot belly and clicked to himself. Then he turned and peered outward into the clearing again. He stopped in surprise.

There was something big and shiny in the clearing! He was not sure what he was seeing and being the great hunter that he was, he knelt on hands and knees for a better view the beast. The Pygmy then rose to a standing position and pulled a poisoned arrow from his quiver. Silently he nocked it in his bow. Taking careful aim, he let the missile fly. It flew true, hitting the huge silver thing in the side and splintering before falling to the ground.

N'Geeso frowned. That should not have happened! The little Kamazila chief was perplexed. He rubbed his chin and frowned some more. Perhaps he should hit it with another arrow. Then he made a clicking sound with his tongue and teeth.

"Ki-Gor should know about this," he muttered. "I shall go tell him!"

N'Geeso took one more look at the big silver bird sitting quietly in the clearing. Then he turned and disappeared into the dark jungle. The heat was all but forgotten.

The Pygmy climbed into the trees to make his way back toward the home of Ki-Gor and his mate, Helene. But on a sudden whim he climbed to the very top of the tree he was in, his light weight allowing him to reach the pinnacle. There he had an unobstructed view of the giant silver bird on the ground. He nodded knowingly, agreeing with himself that it was, indeed, a giant bird that sat on the forest floor.

N'Geeso dropped to the lower, cooler levels and, monkey-like, began moving through the trees. He swung on branches and occasionally on vines when those jungle ropes were secure enough to hold his weight.

The Kamazila chief moved steadily through the trees and in a couple of hours, he stood on the brink of a cliff looking out toward an island located in the middle of a roaring river. A tall baobab tree stood directly in the middle of the two acre land mass and near the top, if one looked carefully, could be seen the outline of the jungle man's domicile. N'Geeso could see no activity in the home of his friend and he hoped he was there. He knew of several places in the jungle where the huge white man made his nest, so he could never be sure just where he would find him.

The Pygmy moved down the high river bank a short ways to a swinging vine bridge that he and his men had constructed for Ki-Gor and Helene. The construction of the crossing was sturdy, even though it did much swinging when it was being used.

Once on the island, N'Geeso gave a chirping bird call. This he repeated several times before he heard a reply and his face broke into a smile. His big friend was on the island. Then he frowned. The reply did not sound exactly as he had expected.

He had been on the trail that led to the big baobab tree where the home of his friends had been constructed. Now he stepped back in the shadows and then, without a sound, swarmed up the tree. He would wait and see who came along the trail.

Presently he saw Ki-Gor's mate, Helene, step into view and come down the trail. She was dressed in leopard skin trunks and top. Over her shoulder hung a bow and quiver full of arrows. In her right hand, she carried an *assegai*, very similar to what the jungle man would carry, but much lighter.

N'Geeso smiled. He had helped teach the white mate of his friend how to use the bow and arrow and he was quite pleased with how rapidly the woman had become proficient with the weapon. His only concern was the redheaded female refused to use poison on the arrows, saying it was not something she was comfortable in handling.

Helene came to a stop, her *assegai* held ready, as she heard the Pygmy coming down the tree. Then she smiled at the little man.

"Welcome, N'Geeso!" she exclaimed. "What brings you to our island?"

"I have news for my friend, Ki-Gor," said the Kamazila chief. "Would Ki-Gor be about somewhere?"

"He is presently gone," replied Helene. "Is the news urgent?"

"That, one does not know," N'Geeso replied, clicking his teeth as he spoke. "I thought perhaps my big brother would know."

"He went down to the great swamp," replied Helene. "I did not go because I do not like the mosquitoes down there! They must be the largest anywhere in the world."

"I have seen most of the world," replied N'Geeso, "and I can say with much truthfulness, they are as large as any you will find anywhere."

"They do not seem to bother Ki-Gor much," said the girl ruefully, "but every time I go down there with him, they try to devour me immediately."

"That is a two day journey," said N'Geeso. "Is it about time for his return?"

Helene shook her head slowly. "He has had about enough time to get there," she said. "It will be several days yet before he returns."

N'Geeso frowned and shook his head, causing his brass earrings to bounce. "I think he would want to know what I have to say," the chief said between clicks of his tongue and teeth.

Helene smiled slightly, thinking how not long ago she would have had no clue as to what the little man was saying. Now, she was rather adept at deciphering his speech.

"You could tell me," she said, "and I could pass the information on when he returns."

The dark man screwed up his face momentarily and then he broke into a smile. "Yes," he nodded. "That would be best now."

"And what is this news that Ki-Gor should hear?" asked Helene when the Pygmy hesitated.

"I saw a silver bird," the chief said slowly.

He saw a bird! Helene thought, struggling to keep from laughing. Ki-Gor would certainly be interested in this!

"It was big!" the little man said, spreading his arms. "He was resting in a clearing! I shot him with a poisoned arrow! It bounced off and he never moved! Ki-Gor must see this creature!"

"Did the bird make any noise?"

"No, he was silent. Like death, but I am sure he was alive," said N'Geeso.

"And how big did you say this bird was?" asked Helene, beginning to wonder just exactly what it was they were talking about.

"Very big!" exclaimed the little man. "From where we are now standing," he said, "to that tree over there."

"Say, that is large!" exclaimed the girl. "Did this bird have feathers?"

"I could not say," said N'Geeso. "But he did have whiskers sticking out of his beak!"

"Did this bird have eyes?"

"Oh, yes! They were large, but not shaped like a normal eye." The chief measured out a square for Helene with his arms. "I think they may have bulged out a little bit, too," he added.

"What about his wings?" she asked. "Were they folded back against his body?"

"No, no," the Pygmy said, clicking his teeth. "They were stretched out, like he was in flight. I thought, if he saw me, he might gobble me up!"

Helene was silent for a moment. Then she looked back at N'Geeso. "Could you take me to see this bird?" she asked.

The Pygmy chief shrugged. "If you wish to see such a terrible creature," he said.

"How long will it take us to get there?" she asked.

The chief pointed at the sun. "From there to there," he said.

"About two hours, I think," the woman replied. "Can we start now?"

"If you are ready," he said.

Helene was aware the little man would very likely travel through the trees, much like a monkey. From a small packet at her waist, she took out a cord which she fastened about the head of her *assegai*. Then she slipped her head and left arm through the loop and the weapon lay neatly on her back, right up against her quiver of arrows.

They climbed a huge tree, crossed the swinging bridge, and started west through the jungle using the tree route. N'Geeso did not race, but he did not move slowly as they swung through the trees on their way to see the silver bird.

From the size of it and from N'Geeso's description, Helene was beginning to believe he had seen some type of airplane, but she could not, of course, be sure until she saw it.

They traveled silently and Helene's thoughts ran back to the time when she was trying to set a record solo flight from the west coast to Nairobi. Something had gone wrong with the engine of her sleek monoplane and she went down quickly. She had had the good sense to dump the large fuel supply she was carrying in an effort not to have a huge blaze when she slammed into the thick jungle. Then at the last moment, an open area appeared and she tried to get her landing gear down as she banked toward it. One of the wheels caught a tree top, tilting the plane. A wing brushed something and spun her sideways. She was careening downward too fast and the monoplane felt like it was tumbling. That was the last she knew.

When she came to her senses, she was sitting in the grass not far from the wreckage of her twisted, mangled airplane. She was just regaining her composure when she heard a sound and turned immediately. The young woman found herself facing a black panther, moving toward her through the grass.

She struggled to regain her feet, but she was going to be easy pickings for the large cat. Then she saw Ki-Gor for the first time as he intercepted the panther. The giant white man slew the panther with his knife in the ensuing battle.

Helene smiled at the memory. How her life had changed from that point forward.

Suddenly she realized she was right beside N'Geeso and the man was signaling for her to remain quiet. The woman immediately became motionless as she strained to hear or see what had brought her companion to a halt.

Then she could make out the trail not far below them and as she watched, she saw a black warrior moving along it. The Pygmy and the white woman would remain perfectly still and the fellow on the path would never know they were just above him.

N'Geeso and Helene were absolutely silent and motionless. The warrior was a Wunguba and he would never have discovered the two people above him, but perhaps they were too quiet.

The figures in the tree remained motionless as the man came up the trail. The stillness convinced a Lusula monkey to make an attempt at pilfering an egg from an open nest of a pair of Black-billed Turacos. The birds were on the thief immediately, squawking and cawing loudly. With terrified shrieks, the monkey fled, but the damage was done.

The Wunguba looked up immediately and he just happened to be lined up where he could see the shadowy shapes of the two humans.

"Hai!" the black cried and quickly reared back and hurled his spear up into the tree.

N'Geeso and Helene had immediately ducked behind the bole of the tree. The iron head of the spear stuck deeply into the tree trunk. Then N'Geeso stepped out with a drawn bow and sent a poisoned arrow into the chest of the man who was beginning to climb the tree.

A bewildered look crossed the fellow's face. Then he dropped back to the ground where he began to convulse violently. In moments he was dead.

N'Geeso dropped down and removed his arrow, all the while watching should others of the warrior's band happen to appear. None did.

The Pygmy quickly climbed back into the tree. He worked the dead man's weapon out of the bole of the tree and dropped it on the ground beside the corpse.

"Silly to throw your weapon into a tree," the Kamazila chief commented.

"Ki-Gor has always said the Wunguba were not a smart people," agreed Helene.

"We go," said N'Geeso. They immediately began moving through the branches of the forest. Helene felt as if she had renewed energy after the incident with the Wunguba warrior.

As they traveled, the woman began to think back to the time she had entered Ki-Gor's world, leaving her own position in high society behind her.

Not only was she an excellent pilot, but she had also excelled in the sport of swimming and diving. A brief smile flitted across her face as she recalled how she had entertained hopes of making the Olympic team to compete in the Berlin Olympics. She wondered just how far out of shape she was and what it would take to once again become competitive.

Then she chuckled, just loud enough that N'Geeso looked back to see why she was making the noise. She just smiled and waved. They continued onward.

Helene decided that she might not be as far out of shape as she thought. After all, she was far stronger and much more agile than she had ever been in her life. Living in the jungle had redirected what she thought of as being important. She was now very proficient in throwing her *assegai*, both for distance and for accuracy. She was also very adept in using her bow and arrows. She wondered how she would fare if she were to enter events in track and field or in archery. She decided she would probably never know.

She was aware that since she and Ki-Gor swam almost daily and she had several places where she could dive into their natural pool, that she was very likely in the best shape of her life and wasn't even aware of it! Helene smiled to herself.

N'Geeso had come to a stop. Helene moved up beside him as he pointed through a break in the trees to an open area. The woman with the dark red hair looked and then gave a gasp.

"The bird is big, is it not?" whispered N'Geeso. "It must be very tired for it is still resting."

"N'Geeso," said Helene in a low voice, "that is not a bird but a flying machine made by the white people."

The Pygmy turned toward the young woman with a slight frown on his face.

"Have you seen anyone around it?"

"No," replied the Pygmy chief. "He has just rested where he landed."

"Did you see him land?" asked Helene quickly.

"No, no," the man said, shaking his head. "He was already roosting when I saw him!"

The woman quickly descended the tree. Then, checking the clearing carefully before leaving the safety of the jungle, she stepped out and moved toward the airplane. As she walked, she removed the assegai and carried it in her right hand. N'Geeso remained in the shadows of the forest.

Helene Vaughn walked quickly and quietly to the plane resting silently in the open space in the jungle. "It is a high-wing craft," she murmured to herself as she approached, "and single-engine. I wonder why they came down here. Perhaps they are out of petrol."

She approached the side and reached out to touch the compressed wood that made up the slick white plane. It had been varnished to a high luster, making it shine like silver in the sunlight. Helene was impressed with the workmanship.

The young woman walked all the way around the airplane observing it from all angles. She could detect nothing that appeared to be wrong with it. She walked around it a second time and could feel the thrill and excitement building within her. She had so loved to fly!

Moving up to the side of the plane, she could see the door was not latched and her heart jumped at the chance to look inside. Quickly she tugged the door open and, placing the assegai just inside the door, proceeded to lift herself into the airplane. The interior had room for six passengers in addition to the pilot.

Helene was very quiet as she stood motionless and looked about to make sure there was no one else on the flying machine. Satisfied, she then went to the door and called for N'Geeso.

The Pygmy chief advanced slowly toward the huge bird setting on the jungle floor.

"Come inside," she called when the little man was closer. "This is a flying machine. It is somewhat like the one I was flying when I crashed in the jungle. Mine, however, was a monoplane meaning it would carry only the pilot. This one appears to seat six people. I wonder where they are?"

N'Geeso cautiously entered the plane. His eyes were big as he looked about the interior and he was very quiet.

"Look!" came Helene's excited voice from the cockpit. "An instruction booklet! Not so much on how to fly this baby but more on how to take care of it! This is a Lockheed Vega! And from the looks of things, I believe I could fly it!"

She sat down in the pilot's seat and began looking at the controls and instruments. The Pygmy came and looked over her shoulder, although he had no idea what Helene was looking at.

"Yes," she said, after a few moments, "I am sure I could fly this plane, especially if it has a good supply of petrol."

"Well," came a strange voice, "you are the answer to our prayers!" Helene froze and her blood ran cold.

Turning quickly, she saw two men with drawn handguns facing her. N'Geeso was reaching to draw his belt knife.

"N'Geeso, no," she said in a voice that quavered. "Do not draw your knife. These people may be friendly." This was spoken in Swahili which the little Pygmy understood much better than the English the woman was teaching him.

"I am sorry for entering your airplane," she said, reverting back to the English she had been speaking when the two men had overheard her. "I used to fly and was very excited to see an airplane again! And the door was unlatched…"

"You certainly don't look like any pilot I ever saw," said the first man.

"How much experience have you actually had?" the second man questioned her.

Helene rose from the pilot's seat and both men stared at the statuesque figure before them, dressed only in a loin cloth and a halter. She placed one hand on N'Geeso's shoulder to reassure the little man.

"I know enough about flying," she said, "to know that it was really foolish to set your plane down right here. It may be very difficult to take off again."

"Well, we didn't have much choice," said the first man.

"If you're such a good flier," said the second fellow, "just who are you? We may have heard of you." He snickered as if he had just cracked a joke.

"I am Helene Vaughn," replied the jungle woman. "My plane went down not too far from here. I was fortunate to have survived."

"I thought you were a good pilot," said the second man, still snickering.

"Helene Vaughn?" questioned the first man. "I've heard of you! And I do recall reading about you disappearing on a flight across the Congo or equator or something like that! I thought they had given up on ever finding you."

"I came back," said Helene. "It was in the papers and on the air waves! You probably just missed it."

"I'm Josh Martin," said the first man. "It is really nice to make your acquaintance. You very possibly might be able to help us out."

"Nice to meet you, Mr. Martin,"

"I am the president of Bander Goods Incorporated. This is my vice president of the corporation, Mr. Dale Drennon."

The second in command nodded at Helene, but did not speak. Neither man had offered to shake hands.

"What brings you to my jungle?" asked Helene. "And, if the plane is still in good flying order, why did you set down here?"

"That is a rather confusing story, which I shall tell you shortly. However, right now we have an injured man over at the edge of the jungle and we'd like to get him on board the plane."

"Injured?" question the woman. "What happened to him?"

"We are not sure," Josh Martin replied. "We were returning to our plane a short time ago. Rowdy, who is our pilot, stepped on a stick that broke. We all heard it snap, but a piece of it stuck in his leg. He pulled it out and threw it away."

"You didn't see the stick?" asked Helene.

"No, Rowdy said he'd be alright, that it was just a small scratch," said the man. "But it began to swell and Rowdy broke out in a sweat. Now, I know it is hot out there, but the sweat was just running off of him in rivulets! He began breathing heavy and fast. There is a river over there about half a mile or so, and we took him there to bathe him. Thought the water might help. He was in really bad shape by the time we got him there, but the water did seem to help. We decided we'd better get him back here to the plane and see if we could get airborne again. When we reached the edge of the jungle, we could see that someone was inside our machine. We figured it was natives being curious and we'd just scare them off."

"Your pilot is at the edge of the jungle?" asked Helene. "May we take a look at him? There might be something we could do."

"Sure," said Josh Martin, holstering his pistol. "He is right over there with Berta."

"Berta?" questioned Helene.

"Yeah, she is Rowdy's girl friend and he insisted on bringing her along. Kind of a mixed blessing, that woman! She's been both a help and a hindrance."

Josh Martin led the way off the Lockheed Vega, followed by Helene, who picked up her assegai by the door. Behind her was N'Geeso and the last one out was Dale Drennon who still held his pistol in his hand. The group walked around the plane to the opposite side.

Led by Martin, they strode quickly toward the forest. When they stepped out of the clearing into the semi-darkness of the jungle, they came upon a woman holding the form of a man and rocking gently back and forth, tears streaming down her face.

"How is he, Berta?" asked Martin.

The woman shook her head. "I think Rowdy has died," she said in a raspy voice.

Martin and Drennon stood staring at the form of their pilot being held in the arms of the woman. Helene moved over and knelt by Berta's side. She checked for a pulse but could find none. Then she looked at the swollen leg of the man. N'Geeso came to stand beside her.

"The man is dead," said the Kamazila chief. "Poison from arrow."

"Was he shot by a Pygmy?" whispered Helene, using Swahili and hoping the white men would not understand the language.

"No," said N'Geeso. "He just suffered a scratch. If the arrow had stuck in him very deeply, he would have died quickly."

Helene remembered the Pygmy chief saying he had shot the big bird once with an arrow and it had just bounced off. The pilot had evidently stepped on it and suffered a light scratch, perhaps just enough for the arrow to break the skin above his boot top.

"What do we do now?" sobbed Berta.

"We can't put him on the plane," said Drennon. "The odor would be bad before we could get back to civilization!"

"We need to bury him here," said Martin. "We've got a couple of shovels on the plane, so we might as well get started."

Berta was sobbing uncontrollably. Helene stepped over and placed an arm about her shoulders. That was when she realized how broad across the shoulders the woman was.

Martin and Drennon came back with shovels and began digging not far from the spot where the pilot had died. They had difficulty with roots and finally decided on a shallow grave. Helene suggested they cover the freshly dug burial spot with rocks to keep animals from digging it up. They two men were tired from digging and did not want to carry rocks.

Helene and N'Geeso helped Berta carry a number of large stones and place them on the gravesite.

Darkness had fallen and with the coming of night, Martin and Drennon had started a campfire and brought out some food.

"If you can fly that plane," said Martin, "we are certainly in need of your services. We will pay you quite well."

"Can you fly?" asked Helene, turning to the stocky Berta Zinger.

The woman shook her head negatively. "Rowdy was teaching me, but all I have done is control it in flight. I could not take off or land. No, I can't pilot it."

Martin and Drennon began digging…a shallow grave.

Helene turned to N'Geeso. "I may need to fly these people out of here," she said in Swahili. "I want you with me as I do not yet trust them."

Speaking of trust, the tall redheaded woman was not sure one or both of the two white men might be able to either speak or understand Swahili. With that thought in mind, she tried to garble her speech so that it would be difficult to understand, even if one were fluent in Swahili. She even mixed in a few clicks such as N'Geeso might do in speaking the Kamazili tongue.

The Pygmy chief smiled at Helen's attempt to disguise her speech, but he knew what she was trying to do and said nothing.

The three strangers went to the safety of the airplane to spend the night, but before going, Martin got Helene to promise that she would still be there in the morning to fly the plane.

"I will be here because I want to fly it!" she exclaimed. "But I must insist that N'Geeso accompany me. If you won't allow him to go with me, then I won't fly it."

At that comment, Drennon pulled out his hand gun again. And Helene saw Martin signal for the man to put it back in his holster. Helene felt that she was right not to trust them.

"The little man is welcome," assured Martin. "He just needs to stay out of the way."

Once the strangers had gone to the plane for the night, Helene told N'Geeso what to expect when they took flight on the following day. The Pygmy had seen airplanes fly over the jungle previously, but he had never been up close to one, let alone inside the belly of the thing! He was aware that they made a loud noise, although that, too, had always been far away.

"I need you with me," said Helene, "because I do not trust these people. You are to be my eyes watching them while I work all the controls that make the bird fly!"

The little man clacked his tongue in happiness. "You just called it a bird," he grinned.

"Yes," replied the redhead with a smile, "that is a slang term often used by people working in and around airplanes."

"Huh," grunted the Pygmy, "good slang!"

Helene and N'Geeso were awake and up from the nests, where they had slept in the trees. long before there was any activity from the Lockheed Vega.

"Maybe they all stepped on the broken arrow," said N'Geeso, "and they are dead now!"

"No," smiled Helene, "many white people, such as these, sleep long beyond sunrise."

"Why?" asked N'Geeso. "They miss the best part of the day!"

"True, they do," agreed the woman. "They are in the habit of staying up long hours after the sun has gone down. When they go to bed, the night is half gone, or more!"

"Huh," grunted the little man. "My people would only stay up that late if we were planning a war!"

Helene and N'Geeso found a large branch about twenty feet above the jungle floor where they could sit in the shade and watch the plane. The limb was large enough to make a good sitting place where they would be comfortable. They talked of many things while they waited.

The Pygmy chief was stretched out flat on the branch when a large bug, about the size of his thumbnail, began crawling up his leg. He watched the insect until it came within reach. Then he quickly picked it up and popped it into his mouth. There were three chewing movements of his jaw and then he swallowed.

"Agh," said Helene softly, "I still cannot eat a live bug! Ki-Gor used to eat them quite often but I have convinced him it makes me feel sick when he does that. So he doesn't do that anymore! Thank goodness!"

Then the redhead saw the little man rocking in silent laughter.

"N'Geeso! Why are you laughing?" she demanded.

"Ki-Gor smart," the little man said with a chuckle.

"What do you mean? What are you trying to say?" Helene demanded.

N'Geeso shrugged his shoulders, a movement Helene thought he had picked up from Ki-Gor. "Ki-Gor not eat bugs where woman can see him," he stated.

"You mean he still eats bugs?" demanded the woman, smiling at her companion. Some how she knew that was exactly what was happening.

At that moment, the door of the plane opened and the two men stepped out and made their way into the jungle. A few minutes later, they reappeared and the stocky woman went into the bush.

"They should be about ready to takeoff," commented Helene, as she and the Pygmy began clamoring to the ground.

"Remember," she said softly, as they walked toward the Lockheed Vega, "you watch carefully what these people do while I am flying. Speak to me in Swahili and put in a few clicks so they will not be sure just what you have said."

"You think maybe they understand Swahili?"

"Maybe," the woman replied. "Make it hard for them to know what you said, if you can."

The Pygmy chuckled softly.

"I think," the young woman continued, "we will be flying east, toward the sun. Most likely they will be going to Nairobi, I hope, because I am familiar with that location."

Helene checked the plane over thoroughly, much to the disgust of the two men who wanted to get underway immediately.

"If you are in such a hurry to leave," said Helene pointedly, "you could have been up a little sooner! N'Geeso and I have been waiting for at least two hours and maybe closer to three! And I will check this plane over or I won't even attempt to lift it off the ground!"

Josh Martin and Dale Drennon stopped their fussing, although they waited impatiently.

"Rowdy always checked everything very carefully, too," said Berta to Helene.

"If you find a pilot that doesn't check his plane over carefully," said the redhead, "don't fly with him!"

Berta laughed softly and nodded.

Before long the plane was running and they were all loaded. Helene taxied to the point where she could turn around and takeoff into the wind.

The grassy strip, that looked so smooth from the air or from the treetops, was in reality a rather rugged strip to be landing a plane on or to be taking off.

The sound of the engine was deafening and as the Lockheed Vega gathered speed, the ride was quite bumpy. Finally when they were off the ground, the roughness stopped and they sank back into their seats as the plane climbed. No one had actually said anything and Helene turned the plane into the sun and headed east toward Nairobi.

Minutes went by and the people in the cabin of the plane were silent. Finally, Josh Martin spoke up.

"Helene Vaughn," he said, "just where are you going?"

"Nairobi," the woman replied. "It is the nearest large population center and I am familiar with the airport there."

"No, we don't want to go there. In fact, we can't go there. We are to go to Alexandria as we have contacts there."

"I don't think you have enough fuel to make it to Alexandria," said Helene. "You have just about doubled the distance. Why can't you go to Nairobi?"

"Well, it is a mixed up story with a lot of misunderstanding. I am not liked there and I think they would arrest me, if they could find me there!"

"Can you pick another place? One that is somewhat closer? How about the west coast? That would be closer than flying all the way to the Mediterranean Sea."

"Are you familiar with the west coast of Africa?" Martin asked.

"Yes, somewhat. Enough to fly there and land," Helene replied.

"Okay," said Martin thoughtfully, "go there."

"Something else that has not been brought up," said Helene, as she banked the plane and turned west. "I assumed that since you were stranded in the middle of thousands and thousands of square miles of wilderness, and I was your only hope of flying out, you would see to it that I would be flown back to my homeland?"

"Are you referring to America or to that exhaustively hot jungle?"

"The jungle," replied Helene. "That is where my home is and where my husband is!"

There was silence for a few moments. Then Helene throttled the plane down a slight bit and began turning back toward the area where they had first landed.

"Hey! What are you doing?" demanded Josh Martin.

"Going back to the clearing," said Helene. "N'Geeso and I will get out and go home. You can do whatever you like."

"No, no!" exclaimed Josh Martin, his face turning a pale color. "We'd all die there in that balmy jungle! You can't do that to us! Please!"

"If we go to the west coast," said Helene, "you will rent a plane and hire a pilot to fly us back to the spot where you picked us up. Right?"

The woman was still flying back to the original takeoff clearing.

"Okay! Yes, we'll do that!" agreed Josh Martin.

"Good," said Helene, "because the more we keep changing directions, the more fuel is wasted. Now, I am turning west once again. The next time I make a turn it will be to return to the clearing where N'Geeso and I can go home."

"Yes, yes," the man agreed.

An hour passed and the cabin had been relatively quiet. Then suddenly Josh Martin broke the silence. "Down there!" he exclaimed. "Down there! That is the valley we could not find! That is it! I know it is!"

"What are you talking about?" asked Helene.

All three of the passengers were craning to see out the small windows and at the same time, they were all talking at once.

"Wait, wait!" exclaimed Josh Martin. "We've got to make another pass over that valley! I'm just sure that matches exactly with the map I've got!" The man was digging into his pocket and finally produced a folded sheet of paper.

"Right, Boss," said Dale Drennon, "it looks like you've hit pay dirt. That has to be the Valley of Bones."

"It is shaped right," said Berta Zinger, who was not displaying quite the amount of enthusiasm as the two men.

"What are we looking at?" Helene asked again.

"Make another pass over the valley," said Martin, "and then we've got to look for a place where we can land!"

"You are pushing it very close, Mr. Martin," said the pilot. "If you keep making all these rash decisions, I'm going back to meadow where N'Geeso and I will return to our homes! Now, tell me, why the sudden interest in the valley?"

"This was the goal of our original expedition," the man said with a big grin on his face. "We were searching for what has been called the Valley of Bones! It is a horseshoe shaped valley that has only been visited by one other group. And out of that group, only one man lived to tell the tale."

"And that guy is now dead," said Berta.

"There is wealth down there," chortled Josh Martin. "Enough to make us all rich beyond our wildest dreams!"

"We'd better get this plane turned around," growled Dale Drennon, "and get to looking for a place where we can set down!"

"Helene, we've got to turn back," said Martin. "We need to find a landing spot and then we can look for the treasure!"

"Treasure?" questioned Helene.

"The surviving member of the first expedition," gloated Martin, "came back with a large number of gold coins! He said this valley was full of all kinds of treasure!"

"And you don't think the natives, who own it, will have any say in what happens to their gold coins?" asked Helene, a bit of sarcasm in her voice.

"Oh, the old fellow claimed there were no people in the valley! Hadn't been for a long time. He said there was all kinds of wealth! Gold, silver, jewels, just everything! We've got to go back and check this out!" gushed Martin. "I've got a lot tied up in this expedition and I really need to make a success out of this trip!"

Helene nodded and began turning back toward the Valley of Bones. From the altitude of the plane, it was easy to see the horseshoe shape of the valley. The woman moved the craft over to one point of the shoe shape and began to follow it.

"I would guess," said Helene, "the entire valley is about ten miles long and varies anywhere from half a mile to a mile in width."

Both Martin and Drennon were nodding in agreement.

"Could we get a little lower?" asked Martin. "Maybe we could see a good place to land."

Helene dropped the plane lower until they were just a short distance above the tree tops in the valley. This put the Lockheed Vega on about the same level as the surrounding jungle above the valley. There was a fairly large river flowing through the depression and they could see where the water created a falls coming into the area. At the opposite end, some ten miles from the falls, was a small lake. There did not seem to be an outlet for the water.

"I wonder why the whole canyon hasn't filled up with water?" asked Berta Zinger.

"Very likely," replied Helene when it seemed no one else was going to offer an explanation, "…there is a place where it runs out at the bottom of the lake. If there is, there should be a river on the other side that just appears from nowhere and begins flowing onward."

With that, Helene lifted the plane up and out of the valley. She maneuvered the craft so that it was near the end of the valley where the lake was, but on the outside. In just moments they all saw the water flowing away from the base of the cliffs that surrounded the valley. Then not far, perhaps a mile, the water gathered, forming another lake. This one was somewhat larger than the lake inside the canyon valley.

"By golly, you were right, Helene," said Martin. "How'd you happen to know that?"

"I may have crashed my plane in the jungle," said the young woman softly, "but I am not stupid. I have an education. On top of that, I have seen similar formations in nature. That, and some good guess work," she laughed.

"I saw nothing down in the valley that even resembled a decent place to set down," she said, winging back toward the center of the horseshoe.

"No," agreed Martin. "There was nothing there. But we really need to land so we can do our search of the valley."

Helene lifted the plane up and over the central area of the horseshoe. While most of the area was covered with vegetation, there were places devoid of forest growth. Helene checked them all over carefully before deciding on which one to use as a landing strip.

Martin, Drennon and Zinger were all anxious to get on the ground and get started toward what they thought was fantastic wealth for the taking.

Once they had landed, Martin unlocked a storage compartment and handed his two companions large caliber rifles. And he had one for himself. Helene noticed there was still one gun in the storage bin, but assumed that had been for the deceased pilot, Rowdy Garfield. Next, the man gave each member a backpack, which they immediately shouldered.

"I wonder which way would be the best direction to go to get down in the valley?" questioned Martin, not really expecting anyone to answer him. The group of three were now standing outside the plane.

"From this location," said Helene, "I would suggest you go straight to the lower edge of the inside of this horseshoe. There, many of the rocks have slid down the side and you should be able to make your way down without too much trouble."

"How do you..." Drennon started to ask before Helene broke in.

"I saw it from the air," she said. The man glared at Helene. His obvious dislike for her was beginning to surface more and more. Helene assumed it was because she could fly the plane, while he could not.

"Let's go," said Martin, turning toward the lower tip of the horseshoe.

"I believe N'Geeso and I will just stay here," said Helene. "We can keep an eye on the plane."

Martin grumbled something and then stalked back and locked the door of the Lockheed Vega. Helene was surprised but did not show any resentment at the implication she could not be trusted.

"Just so you and your buddy don't decide to leave us stranded out here," he snapped at the young woman.

"Good luck," smiled Helene as the three treasure hunters hurried away. None of them seemed to have heard her.

"Did the man fasten the door?" asked N'Geeso.

"Yes, he locked it," replied Helene.

"We cannot get in? If we could, we could just fly off and leave these people. They do not belong in the jungle. And the jungle will take care of them."

Helene walked over and tried the door. The handle would not move.

"We can not get in, can we?" asked N'Geeso.

"I think we can," smiled Helene, "but let's give them time to get farther away."

They waited for several minutes and then Helene reached into the small packet that she carried on her belt and lifted out a key.

"Do you think that will open the door?" the Pygmy asked.

"I don't know," the woman replied. "It was hanging on the dash when I got into the pilot's seat and there did not seem to be a place to use it in flying, so I am guessing it might open the door."

They tried the key and the door opened immediately.

"There is something else I want to try," she said. "You stay out here and watch for their return. I don't want them to catch me doing this."

N'Geeso nocked an arrow and stood guard outside the plane while Helene entered. She went directly to the storage compartment and tried the handle. It was locked, as she had assumed. She tried the key and grinned when it opened that compartment as well. She looked at the items stored there, which included the fourth rifle and many boxes of ammunition. There were some papers and maps, along with a fourth backpack and a medical kit. But she did not want to disturb anything, so she did not touch them. She closed and locked the storage unit.

"N'Geeso," she said, stepping outside the plane, "let's go see what lies beyond the jungle." She turned and locked the door. Then she replaced the key to her belt packet.

Quietly, the Pygmy and the jungle girl walked away from the plane.

When they arrived at the rock slide, there was a trail already there leading down into the Valley of Bones. N'Geeso checked it over carefully.

"Those three went down here," he said. "But this is not an animal path. This trail was made by people coming and going from this place."

"Yes," nodded Helene. "Martin said this place was uninhabited, but as soon as he said it, I thought he had lied to us. He was aware there were people here and he is prepared to take their wealth from them."

"He is a bad man," said N'Geeso.

"I think he is a gangster," the young woman said. "That is just another name for a bad man," she added, upon seeing the Pygmy's bewildered look.

"Gangster!" repeated N'Geeso, nodding with a fierce look on his face. "N'Geeso may have to put arrow in gangster!"

Helene laughed lightly and they started down the winding trail.

It did not take long to reach the bottom.

"They went that way," said N'Geeso, pointing to the left.

"Then we should go this way," said Helene, starting to her right.

"Yes," said the Pygmy, "we do not want to be with the gangster when he does evil things!"

Helene chuckled softly as she fell in behind the little man leading off to the right on a trail that led in both directions from the twisting path on the rock slide.

They started down the winding path.

It was obvious that N'Geeso was feeling really good now that he was out of the flying bird. There was a bounce in his step and Helene thought he would be singing, if his people did that sort of thing.

Suddenly the little man stopped, his hand upraised as he listened. Helene strained to hear as well, but nothing came to her.

"This way," whispered N'Geeso.

They pushed quickly through the jungle brush and in moments came upon a trail that appeared to be seldom used. The Pygmy moved ahead rapidly and Helene followed right on his heels.

Then they left the trail and a moment later burst through the vegetation into an open area that was surrounded on three sides by rock walls. Standing in an alcove with his back against the stone was a teenage boy, holding a lowered spear. At his feet lay his hunting companion in somewhat of a daze with several bloody claw marks across his body.

Facing the two boys was a large leopard, crouched and ready to spring again. N'Geeso wasted no time in raising his bow and sending an arrow into the rear haunch of the cat. The animal snarled and whirled, biting at the stinging barb protruding from his hip joint.

Then the cat's actions slowed entirely and he slumped to the ground. In a few seconds he rolled over, dead.

"We come as friends," called N'Geeso in a language Helene could not understand. He had one hand raised with palm facing the two youngsters.

"Who are you, mighty hunter?" asked the standing lad.

"I am N'Geeso," replied the Pygmy. "I come in peace, but I heard your call and came to help."

"I am Opai," the boy said. "This is my friend Undutu. The cat jumped him before we knew he was there."

"Let us see to his wounds," the little man said. "Perhaps we can help."

He started toward the downed boy and Helene followed closely behind him. Opai knelt by his friend, reassuring him that the two strangers would help him.

Opai looked up at N'Geeso. "I have never seen anyone who could shoot a big cat in the behind hard enough to kill him!"

"Is there water close by?" the Pygmy asked. "We need to clean out these wounds so they will heal properly."

"Fifty paces that way," said Opai, pointing.

N'Geeso went to the leopard and carefully removed his arrow. Carefully, he cleaned it and then replaced it in his quiver. Once that was taken care of, he and Helene lifted the injured boy to his feet. Supporting him from both sides, they followed Opai to a small stream with clear running water. They lay the boy flat on his stomach and went to work cleaning the wounds on his back. They held some of the deeper ones compressed to help stop the bleeding.

"You know what we need," said Helene, "is that first aid kit on the plane! I'm going to go get it! You might see if you can move him closer to that rock slide. I think there is water running close by that trail."

"Watch for the gangsters," warned N'Geeso, and Helene was off and running toward the rock slide and the plane.

She was breathless when she arrived but she quickly got the key out and unlocked the door. She debated on taking the whole kit and then decided to just take the disinfectant as the boy would probably not leave any tape or padding stuck to him.

Helene picked up the bottle of Mercurochrome, replaced the kit and left the plane. She stopped long enough to lock the door and as she turned to race back to N'Geeso and the injured boy, she heard rifle shots.

They came from some distance and were to her left so she was sure it didn't have anything to do with N'Geeso, Opai and Undutu. Josh Martin and his companions had very likely just startled some large animal and, with the mentality of the great white hunter, started blazing away.

Helene estimated that it was just a little past midday and the heat was bearing down. It would be another extremely hot day. However, the rains would come soon, she was sure of that.

She coated all the open wounds on Undutu with the Mercurochrome. He seemed to be feeling better since they had cleaned the wounds with the cold water from the stream emanating from the base of the cliff wall and the medicine would help stop infection.

"Our village is not far," said Opai. "We go to the far wall," and he pointed across the horseshoe shaped valley. "There is a rock slide there and a trail that leads to the top. Our village is a short distance back in the jungle. We should take Undutu there."

"Yes, we should," agreed N'Geeso. "We will help you."

They crossed several streams, none of which were overly large but Helene was aware they would flow together in the center of the canyon and eventually form a nice sized river.

There was a trail that led across the valley and they followed it slowly, with the injured boy leaning on both N'Geeso and Opai. By the time they reached the rock slide, he was feeling well enough that he needed very little support.

They were near the rim of the sunken valley when they heard the shots again and they all stopped to listen. The two boys had quizzical expressions on their faces, but they did not ask N'Geeso if he knew what they were and the Pygmy chief did not offer an explanation.

The boys topped the rim with Undutu moving under his own power.

"It might be best if we did not go into the village," whispered Helene to N'Geeso. "We do not know what the attitude of these people might be. They might insist that we stay for a while and I really would like to get our passengers loaded up and on the way again. We are wasting a lot of time and I am concerned about landing in the dark."

Suddenly a group of a dozen warriors burst from the surrounding jungle, spears leveled at the Pygmy and the white woman. They seemed to feel that the two boys were being held against their will.

Opai went to the fellow who was the leader and spoke quickly. He pointed at N'Geeso and at Helene. Then he stepped over and showed the man the leopard scratches on Undutu. The hardness of the man's face softened and he began nodding gently as the boy told him the story.

At a command from the leader, all the menacing spears were relaxed with the butt of the weapon being lowered to the ground. Both N'Geeso and Helene breathed a sigh of relief.

"A runner came to our village just now," said the leader to N'Geeso. "It seems some strangers are near the temple. That is never good, so we go to help."

"We will walk with you," said N'Geeso. "We would like to see these strangers and your temple. With your permission?"

The leader grunted and nodded. Then he turned to Opai. "Take your friend to the village," he said. "Explain to his mother how he came to have all those claw marks."

There was disappointment on Opai's face as he had hoped he would be allowed to accompany the warriors.

"I am Karpai," the man said, turning back to N'Geeso. "I am the leader of this village. We Kaseesa go to help our cousins who may need us!"

"I am N'Geeso, chief of the Kamazili," said the Pygmy, inflating his chest somewhat as he made the statement. "My companion is Helene, who is the mate of Ki-gor, mighty lord of the jungle. You may have heard of him as he is known far and wide!"

Karpai frowned slightly. "I do not know of this Ki-Gor," he said. Then after a moment's hesitation, he added, "We must hurry to see what is happening with our cousins!"

"We will follow our friends," said the Pygmy as Karpai led his warriors down the rocky slope into the Valley of Bones. N'Geeso and Helene followed closely on their heels. Once they were on the valley floor, they broke into a ground eating trot.

Helene estimated they had covered close to two miles along the right hand bank of the river that wound through the valley, when they broke into an open area. Karpai brought his men to a halt. Before them was another rock slide, one of the many there seemed to be along the walls of the sunken valley. And beyond the jumbled rocks was an open area with sparse vegetation growing intermittently.

The first thing to catch their eyes was the large block building on the opposite side. It had a round shape with a domed roof. Behind it were several other buildings of a similar shape. In front of the buildings was a stone wall about three feet in height that had been covered with the same type of covering on the walls of the buildings. It was some kind of clay or cement-like material and it had been coated with a lighter color, again similar to the buildings.

Helene wondered why they had not been able to see these buildings from the air when they flew over the valley. Then she realized that many of the trees growing around the structures were taller. That would have effectively hidden them from view.

The second thing she and N'Geeso noticed was the thin line of native warriors scattered along the fringes of the open area. None were very close to the buildings or the wall that surrounded them and all of the men seemed to be armed with spears. Upon closer examination, they could see an occasional body sprawled on the ground closer to the domed structures.

"The way those buildings are built," said Helene to N'Geeso, "and the way these warriors are armed suggests two different groups of people."

The Pygmy glanced up at her but did not say anything.

"I am guessing," she continued, "the treasure Martin's group was searching for, was located in those buildings. I also believe he knew exactly where to go to find what he wanted. He wasn't searching for lost treasure, he was planning to rob these people!"

"Gangsters!" commented N'Geeso.

Helene and N'Geeso remained in the shadows of the trees. Subconsciously, she was trying to remain out of sight of the people from the airplane. She already distrusted them.

Karpai gave a verbal command that sounded somewhat animal-like, yet also human. Several of the warriors crouched behind bushes turned to see the dozen Kaseesa warriors. A few were concerned that there was a white woman with them.

Another man came forward to speak with Karpai. Evidently he was the leader of the group that appeared to have some group pinned down behind the stone wall.

"As you know," said the second leader, "we always have a sentinel watching the temple. He sent us word as soon as these thieves appeared. There are only three of them, but they have the magic sticks that can strike from a distance."

"You are too far away to strike them with your spears," broke in N'Geeso. "Perhaps you would allow me to move around to one side and shoot them with an arrow."

The two leaders looked at the four foot Pygmy standing with his short bow and arrows. His small face resembled that of an old monkey and the large dangling earrings did not give him the appearance of a warrior.

"This man saved one of our young warriors from the spotted cat," said Karpai. "He shot it in the rump and it died! Perhaps he can shoot the thieves."

The second man nodded in agreement, but it was obvious he did not think so.

"Where is the best place for me to get above them so that I can shoot downward?" asked N'Geeso. "From here, I cannot even see them."

Karpai screwed up his face and the second leader gave a derisive chuckle.

"Never mind!" N'Geeso snapped. "I find for myself!"

The Pygmy turned and moved away. When the two men glanced back again to see where he was going, he was out of sight. They did not know where he was.

They conferred for a few minutes and then decided to do another charge. This tactic had not been particularly successful, but they did not know what else to do.

The Kamazili Pygmy looked for and found a huge tree that towered above the buildings. Quickly, he scurried up the trunk until he had a height where he could look down on the three gunmen behind the wall. He settled into place and got his bow and arrows ready for use.

As soon as the spearmen launched their charge, the three figures behind the stone wall stood up and began firing their rifles. They had no fear of the spears as the natives could not throw them that far.

Then Helen's first arrow went whizzing between Josh and Dale. Both men were aware of it and they quickly dropped behind the wall again. The second arrow went through Berta's sleeve drawing blood as it did so. The woman immediately joined the two men on the ground behind the stone wall.

The heavy fire from the three guns was enough to break the charge of the natives. They raced back to the edge of the clearing where there was some cover. The brush would not protect them from the bullets but it did make them hard to see.

As Helene watched, she thought she saw a dark figure moving back among the buildings, but since she could not identify it, she would not shoot. It could be one of the natives or it might have even been N'Geeso.

Time dragged on with an occasional shot being fired from behind the stone wall.

Then came a scream and Dale Drennon stood up straight, clutching at an arrow protruding from his chest. Then he slowly crumpled to the ground.

Following Drennon's death, for the Pygmy poison works very quickly, there came a barrage of gunshots aimed toward the trees off to the right hand side of the buildings. Then things became very silent again.

Two minutes later there came a garbled squawk and Josh Martin reared up on his feet, an arrow protruding through both sides of his neck. Then he fell forward, draped over the wall, just as dead as Drennon.

Helene walked up beside the two native leaders who were staring in disbelief. She cupped her hands to her mouth and called out.

"Berta!" she yelled loudly. "Berta! Come on out! There is no point in dying with Martin and Drennon! Come on out!"

There was no reply.

Suddenly N'Geeso was standing beside the native leaders. "The two gangsters are dead," he said. "I did not see the woman."

"Then she has slipped out," said Helene. There is no one there now."

N'Geeso turned to the two leaders and explained that the enemy was either dead or gone and they could go into the temple yard in safety.

The leaders relayed the information to their warriors, but no one wanted to be the first to walk into the face of what had been sure death.

"I need my arrows," said N'Geeso. "I cannot leave them where someone could accidentally prick themselves. They would die."

"Yes," nodded Helene. The Pygmy and the jungle woman walked out into the open and approached the temple buildings. There was no resistance.

The natives were still reluctant to come forward.

N'Geeso immediately began the careful work of extracting his poison arrows. Helene noticed that both men were missing their backpacks and, with a frown on her face, began checking Josh Martin's pockets for the key to the door of the Lockheed Vega. She could not find it.

"I think," she said, as N'Geeso cleaned his arrows, "that Berta was sent back to the plane with the backpacks and the key. I assume the backpacks were filled with treasure from the temples."

The Kaseesa and their cousins were now gathering at the stone wall.

"Karpai," said N'Geeso, "your problem has been solved. These men came to rob you of your gold and jewels. But they will trouble you no more."

"Ask them to check and see what is missing," whispered Helene. "I am curious as to what Berta may have gotten away with! She is certainly no better than these two men."

N'Geeso made his request and the two leaders started into the first building. Then Karpai motioned for the Pygmy and Helene to follow them. They walked through the first building and then went through three more.

Helene was just stunned at the mass of gold, silver and jeweled items in the four buildings. It was mind boggling and most of the items were placed out where anyone could have lifted them up and taken them away with them. There was an abundance of chalices, all of which were decorated with fine scroll work and inset with glittering jewels. There was also much body jewelry available along with crowns. These, too, were covered with intricate designs and interlaced with many brilliant stones.

"Do they still make these beautiful items?" she asked and N'Geeso put the question to the two men leading them through the buildings. They stopped and talked for several minutes and then finished the check of missing items. Once outside, N'Geeso told the men he and the white woman must be on their way.

"How much was missing?" asked Helene.

"Very little," the Pygmy replied. "They said if we could find the third member of the gangsters and kill her, we could have all the treasure she got away with." The man just shrugged as it all meant nothing to him.

"Do they still make these beautiful items?"

"No," said N'Geeso. "They never made them to begin with. They all came here from trading a long, long time ago. The traders have not come here in the memories of the oldest people in the tribe. No one knows why."

"Did the traders build these buildings?" the woman asked.

"Yes, this is where they stayed when they were here," nodded N'Geeso. "Now, they are just the storage place for the pretty pieces."

"I'm going out on a limb here," said Helene, speaking more to herself than to the Pygmy, "and just guess this was a place where the traders stored their treasure. I really doubt that the natives in the area could have actually produced enough of whatever it was the traders wanted, to obtain all this wealth. Even over a long period of time. I believe the original traders brought it here for safe keeping and the natives were guarding it for them."

Helene looked up at the sun and knew it was mid afternoon. She wasn't sure just where they would go now that Martin and Drennon were no longer in the picture.

The jungle woman and the Pygmy went back to the front of the buildings where they picked up the rifles by the bodies of the two dead men.

"They won't have any use for these anymore," she commented. "We'll take them back with us because I think Tembu George is teaching some of his Masai to use firearms. We'll just turn whatever we end up with, over to him. It will be put to good use that way."

N'Geeso and Helene, each carrying a rifle, walked back to the rock slide with the Kaseesa warriors. They waved, then turned and followed the trail back to the stream, which at this point was becoming larger. Once on the opposite side, it was just a short walk to the rock slide leading up to the Lockheed Vega.

The Kamazili chief looked at the trail and commented, "White woman here already. Maybe in plane."

"I hope she doesn't try to fly it," added Helene.

They arrived at the top of the slide and started through the fringe of trees before reaching the meadow like area where the airplane sat. The first thing they saw was the form of Berta Zinger sitting by the wheel of the craft. From the distance she looked forlorn and defeated.

"What should we do with the guns of the white men?" asked N'Geeso. "Surely the woman will remember that we did not have any."

"I doubt she will remember," said Helene. "She was so excited about getting out and loading up on that treasure, I don't think she'll remember for sure. If she does, we'll just tie her up so she can't do any harm."

When they were closer, the woman scrambled to her feet and came to meet them. Tears were streaming down her cheeks.

"I knew this was a bad deal," she choked out. "Almost everything Josh Martin said turned out to be a lie." She dropped her head as the tears continued to flow.

"So what happened out there?" asked Helene. "We heard a lot of shooting but assumed the men had found a number of animals to shoot at. After all, there are no natives in this area."

"We found the place where the treasure was hidden," sobbed the woman. "But before we could take anything we were attacked by natives! It was horrible!"

"I thought there weren't supposed to be any natives around here," repeated Helene.

"There aren't supposed to be," the woman said. "I think they just happened to discover us there. Maybe they wanted the treasure, too."

"So you did find it, huh?"

The woman nodded and then Helene saw her blood-drenched sleeve.

"Looks like one of them scored a hit," she said. "We need to clean that up and put some medicine on it."

The woman pulled the key out of her pocket and unlocked the door on the plane. Then she put the key back in her pocket and pretended to try getting the storage case opened but it would not budge.

"I guess Josh Martin locked it," she said. "He didn't give me a key for it."

"Oh," said Helene, "is that where the first aid kit is?"

"I think so, if he even has one! I wouldn't put it past him to have skipped on something like that! He wouldn't see any need for it, if he didn't need it right then."

"Him big gangster," commented N'Geeso.

Berta's eyes opened big. "How did you know?" she asked her voice just above a whisper.

N'Geeso just shrugged.

Then the woman turned her eyes to Helene. "When did you know?" she asked again.

The jungle woman also shrugged. "Just a lucky guess. We probably aren't right, though. How long before those fellows will be back, so we can take off?"

"I don't know," she said. "They just told me I should try to get back to the plane."

"Maybe we should take the plane and fly over this place where you found the treasure and see what we can learn," said Helene.

"Oh, I don't want to go back there," she said.

"But what if they are still alive, Berta?"

"Then they can just fend for themselves!"

Helene placed the rifle, her *assegai* and bow and arrows not far from the door of the plane when she entered the craft. Then she went to get the plane started. N'Geeso placed his rifle beside Helene's but he kept his bow and poisoned arrows with him, which he always did.

"So you think you are the only one left?" asked Helene.

"I don't know," said Berta. "I heard a lot of shooting just after I left and then everything got very quiet. Like maybe it was over. So I just don't know."

"Do you think Josh and Dale might show up back here at the plane?

"Honestly, I don't know," the woman said softly. "But I just have the feeling that I am the only one left."

"Would you like for me to send N'Geeso out to check?" asked Helene. "Just to be sure? However, if we do, then we won't be able to leave here until tomorrow sometime."

"Let's go now," Berta said, her body trembling. "I want to get out of here!"

"If you are sure..." began Helene.

"I am sure!" the woman suddenly snapped. "If they had survived, they would have been back here with me! Or at least very shortly afterwords! Those natives got them! I don't know how, but they did. I actually think they brought up an archer! That's how I got the arm wound! And I know Josh and Dale are both dead!"

After that tirade, Helene didn't say word. She just taxied to the point where she could face into the wind and began building up speed. Again, it was rough until they actually left the ground. It was at that point that Helene realized the woman was looking over her shoulder, watching everything she did.

The jungle woman was aware that Berta Zinger had made an earlier comment that her boy friend, Rowdy Garfield, was teaching her to fly. That she could handle the plane while it was in the air but she had no experience either landing or taking off.

Helene was aware that she needed to watch this woman. When the opportunity arose, she would alert N'Geeso.

They had been in the air ten minutes when Berta came up and wanted to know which way they were going.

"We are going back to the spot where you picked up N'Geeso and me," Helene replied.

"Why? I thought we had a deal where you would deliver us to the west coast," the woman said.

"I had a deal with Martin," replied Helene. "He came across as having the money to do what he promised. Now, I'm not sure that he did."

"I could pay you," said Berta.

"We've done enough running back and forth and flying over the Valley of Bones, landing, taking off and all the other little things we've done while we were in the air, that I'm not sure we have the fuel to actually reach the coast now."

...it was rough until...they left the ground

"So what is the plan? You're not just going to dump me in the jungle, are you?"

"No," chuckled Helene. "I wouldn't do that."

Berta Zinger looked almost relieved.

"However," continued the redheaded pilot, "we may have a problem with fuel but my big concern is daylight. We need to land while there is still light for me to see what I am up against. If we can get back to the point where we started this morning, we'll land there. Regardless, if it gets dark I am going to find a place to set down while I can still see what I'm about to hit! I had planned to go a little farther than where you picked up N'Geeso and me. It will be near a Masai village I am familiar with and I have a friend there. He will have fuel brought out by another pilot in another plane. And then this plane can be flown to where ever you want to go. That is, within range of a full tank of fuel."

"It looks like you have it planned out," smiled Berta.

"I try," replied Helene.

They droned on and Helene Vaughn again felt the thrill of flying. N'Geeso sat near her but positioned so that he could see both women. Berta sat a seat farther back and stretched back, becoming drowsy after all the excitement she had been through.

Presently N'Geeso got Helene's attention and nodded to the dozing woman. The jungle woman grinned and motioned the Pygmy forward. She whispered softly in his ear for a moment then quietly moved out of her seat. The Kamazili chief slid silently behind the controls.

"Take hold right here," the woman whispered. "Just hold steady and don't move them."

The little man nodded.

Helene moved silently back by the storage locker. Quietly she removed her key and opened the door just slightly. As she suspected, all three backpacks were stashed inside and all three appeared to be loaded. She nodded and locked the door quietly.

Helene slipped back into the cockpit and traded places with the Pygmy, who had the biggest grin on his face she had ever seen.

"We're carrying a load of treasure," she whispered softly into the man's ear. He nodded as Helene had only confirmed what they both had suspected. Berta snoozed on.

The Lockheed Vega droned eastward and the sun sank closer and closer to the horizon.

"We need to find a place to set this baby down," said Helene calmly. "I don't think we are too far from the spot we left this morning, but we can't take the time to look for it, because if we do and don't find it, that makes me trying to land in the dark. I might as well be blind!"

All three began looking out the windows hoping to see something that looked like a clearing where they could land. It was N'Geeso who saw a spot off to their right and when they turned and passed over it, Helene said it would fill the bill and they would set down immediately.

They made another loop and Helene approached the open meadow with reduced speed. In a few short moments, they were rolling along on the rough terrain and the jungle woman was bringing her craft to a halt.

"That was a good landing, Helene," said Berta. "Someday, I hope to be able to fly as well as you do!"

"Thanks," smiled Helene, "but you must remember I have had a huge number of hours in the air flying. Just not recently."

All three of the fliers were anxious to get out of the plane and stretch their legs. Now that they were on the ground and lower than the tree level they could see that it was getting dark rapidly. Off in the west could be seen a cloud bank above the trees.

"Will it rain tonight?" asked Berta. "It has been so hot lately."

"Well, it could," said Helene. "It can always rain here in the tropics. However, my guess is that it will be a day or two longer and then we will get some really heavy downpour."

"N'Geeso hungry," said the Pygmy.

"Is there food on the plane?" asked Helene.

"There is some canned stuff," said Berta. "Soup, I think. Probably some beans."

Helene explained to the Kamazili Pygmy. N'Geeso screwed up his face and thought for a moment. "I think I go find *jungle bunny*," he finally said.

"I will start a fire and get the coals hot," smiled Helene.

"Where is he going?" asked Berta. "Doesn't he want some food?"

Helene chuckled. "Yes, he wants some food, but your menu did not impress him. He is going out to find a *jungle bunny*."

"*Jungle bunny*? What's that?"

Again, the redhead laughed. "I think that is a term used occasionally by Tembu George, Chief of the M'Balla Masai. N'Geeso and Ki-Gor have both picked it up from him and sometimes use it. A *jungle bunny* simply means a small edible animal in the jungle."

"Like a rabbit or a squirrel?"

"Yes, exactly like that," nodded Helene. "If N'Geeso is lucky and makes a kill quickly, we will each have a piece of fresh roasted meat."

"I think I will go see if there is some canned soup in the tail storage compartment of the plane," the woman said, as she started back to the aircraft.

Helene got the fire started and was feeding it chunks of wood to burn down into hot coals while she wondered if that back storage place was where the shovels had been stored. She looked toward the plane and saw Berta returning. It looked like she had a couple of cans and a pan.

She did, indeed, have a couple of cans of soup and a pan in which to heat it. She had also brought a canteen of water to add to the mixture. She had it warmed thoroughly when N'Geeso came out of the jungle carrying two large fish he had caught."

"No *jungle bunny*?" asked Helene.

"Too dark," the man replied.

"How did you manage to get the fish?" asked Helene. "I didn't think you had a hook or a line."

"I use hands," the man said, as if that were explanation enough.

"Did you go to that small lake we saw as we were landing?" asked Helene.

"Not far," the man nodded.

"I don't think we are very far from where we started," said Helene. "But if it took very much time to find it, it would have been too far. We are just as well off right here."

"N'Geeso smell Wunguba," the Pygmy said.

"You mean right now?" asked Helene, rising to her feet in alarm.

"No," said the little man shaking his head. "In jungle, on trails. Smell them."

"What's he saying?" asked Berta, who realized Helene was taking whatever the information was, very seriously.

"N'Geeso says he has smelled Wunguba in the jungle," replied Helene.

"What is a Wunguba?" asked the stocky woman. "Some kind of man eater?"

"No, the Wunguba is a tribe of natives that do not like white people or missionaries. They killed my husband's father."

"Oh. But they are not around here right now, are they?" asked Berta.

"They have been here recently enough that N'Geeso could smell them," said Helene. "That means fairly recently. And if they are anywhere close, they probably heard the plane come down."

"Good, that means they are probably still running," laughed the woman.

"Either that or they are sneaking up on our camp right now!"

N'Geeso had cleaned the fish, wrapped them in large green leaves and placed them on the hot coals.

Berta poured the soup in the empty cans and offered some to Helene and N'Geeso. The Pygmy leaned over and smelled the fluid without touching the can. Then he shook his head negatively and turned back to tend his cooking fish.

Helene took the proffered can graciously and lifted it to her lips. The soup smelled good and she took a sip. It was good.

"This is good," she said. "N'Geeso, you don't know what you are missing."

"N'Geeso eat fish," the little man said. He had been whittling out some sharp picks while the fish was cooking.

Several minutes later, he removed the fish from the fire and unwrapped the leaves. The steam rolled off the meat and N'Geeso waved his hand back and forth over his baked catch to clear the air.

Then using one of the picks he had whittled out, he stabbed a piece and held it in front of his mouth while he blew on it to cool it off. When it was cool enough, he took a bite and immediately swallowed it.

Then he handed a stick to Helene and one to Berta.

"Blow to cool it," he said.

Helene and Berta both tried the fish and both ate more than one piece.

When they were finished eating, N'Geeso stood up. "I check for Wunguba," he said. Then he disappeared into the shadows of the surrounding jungle.

"What did he say?" asked Berta.

"He is going to check around the clearing and see if he finds any sign of the Wunguba."

"We'll all sleep on the plane, won't we?" asked Berta. "Especially if there natives skulking about out there!"

"I'm sure you will sleep better on the plane," said Helene. "I will sleep in the jungle, up in a tree, and I know that N'Geeso will sleep outside somewhere. He will probably make several checks during the night to see if any Wunguba are around."

"You are both going to sleep out in the jungle?" questioned Berta. "I could see the little guy doing that, but I thought you would want to be inside, especially if there is danger out here."

"Our home is in the jungle," replied Helene and just left it at that.

The woman put out the fire and covered it with sand and loose gravel she could scrape up in the area. Berta watched, but did not offer to help.

Darkness had settled over the jungle and stars were twinkling overhead, except in the far west where the cloud bank rose. A moon would rise shortly.

A dark shadow detached itself from the jungle and moved toward Helene, waiting not far from the covered ashes.

"Anything out there?" she asked very softly.

"They are around, but I did not see anything," N'Geeso replied. "I smell them. I think maybe there is a village not far."

"They probably heard and maybe saw the plane come down," said Helene. "Do you think they will come tonight?"

"They are big cowards," the little man replied. "Maybe they come, maybe not."

Helene nodded. "Berta has gone to the plane. I am not sure she takes this seriously, though. I shall be up in this tree right here," she added.

"I shall sleep in that one," the Pygmy said, pointing to a tree about thirty yards away.

Before long Helene was in her tree, curled up in a huge moss and leaf filled crotch that actually formed a fairly nice bed.

N'Geeso had found a smooth limb running along the edge of the clearing nearly fifty feet off the ground. He stretched out and lay flat on his belly on the limb. This gave him a good view of the clearing and the airplane.

Twice, before midnight, the Pygmy made a circuit of the area. Each time he was satisfied that no Wunguba were close by. This late in the night, he was certain they would not show up and he lay down to sleep on his tree branch.

Noffa the Wunguba lay awake in his mud hut in the village of Retto. He could not sleep because of the anger in his chest. He must do something to impress the father of Nije, the girl of his dreams. They had all heard the great bird fly over the jungle that evening, but not many had the courage to go check it out.

He had suggested to his friend, Netoa, that they go take a look. But Netoa had no interest in seeing the big bird. He had nothing to gain by seeing the creature and everything to lose should the flying beast decide to eat him.

It was two hours past midnight when Noffa decided he just had to go see the bird. His bravery in doing so might win him acceptance by Nije's father. If it were there, he would look just long enough that he could describe the bird to his friends. This should raise his status among the Wunguba and perhaps give him a chance with Nije.

Berta Zinger stretched out on the floor of the plane and was soon asleep. However, in the early morning hours, she found herself awake. She lay there thinking about the treasure she had hidden in the storage compartment of her deceased boy friend's airplane.

Then Berta became a little paranoid as she thought about getting her treasure aboard ship and back to the states with her. She wondered just how much Helene Vaughn and the little Pygmy actually knew.

Her arm ached and she shifted position to relieve the pressure on it. Then her thoughts turned to the fact that she had been scraped by an arrow. The natives they had been shooting at did not seem to have bows and arrows. All they had were spears.

Where did the arrow come from? The only ones with arrows were Helene Vaughn and N'Geeso. Her face screwed up as she determined that one of them had to have shot at her! They were waiting for an opportunity to ditch her! She was sure of it!

Where were they now? Out there in the jungle sleeping in the trees? That, she did not believe. No one would do that. There must be some other reason. They were probably doing something right now to get rid of her! She'd show them! She'd catch them in the act, what ever it was!

Berta got up and quietly slipped out the door. She didn't even think to take her guns with her. She had no idea where she was going, but she headed straight for the jungle. Her stride was long and purposeful. Her face carried a scowl and she marched with a degree of royalty in her mannerism.

The stocky woman burst into the jungle, pushing the brush aside and began looking for the woman and the little man.

Suddenly her head was jerked back and her body was slammed to the turf, knocking the breath from her lungs. She was stunned as she was jerked back on her feet, again by the hair of her head. She gave an uncontrollable squawk and then the haft of a spear slapped across the side of her head and she collapsed again.

The Wunguba village was not far and Neffa was elated with his good fortune. He soon had the woman back on her feet and staggering as he led her through the jungle.

Berta's one cry was enough to awake both Helene and N'Geeso. They were quickly on the ground and moving toward the area from which the sound had come. As they drew closer they could hear some type of activity and they slowed down, entering the forest carefully and quietly.

Neffa struggled somewhat with Berta. He kept a solid hold on her hair and had one hand clapped across her mouth to silence her. He was forcing her ahead of him and they had covered close to a hundred yards.

"Wunguba," came a voice from the darkness, "release the woman!"

Neffa stopped, his eyes wide. "No," he stammered. "She is mine! From the big bird, I took her!"

"Berta," came a feminine voice voice from one side, "relax! Go limp. Go limp!"

The stocky woman finally did as she was told. Neffa couldn't hold her up and she crumpled to the ground.

The next thing Berta knew, the native was collapsing on top of her. Then someone was removing the body, which had an arrow protruding from the chest.

"Hurry," said Helene softly. "Let's get back to the plane!"

Berta mumbled something unintelligible. But Helene grasped her by the hand and they were soon running toward the Lockheed Vega.

The door of the plane had been left open and Helene stuffed the stocky woman inside as quickly as she could. She then picked up the rifle she had earlier placed near the door and turned to face whatever might be following them.

Helene saw nothing, so she took up a position near the front wheels and waited, rifle ready. Presently she was a dark shadow moving across the meadow toward her and recognized it as N'Geeso.

"Did you find anymore Wunguba?" she whispered.

"No, only the one," he replied. "I made a circle. There are no others out there."

"Did you get your arrow?"

"Yes, my arrow is safe," the little man grinned. "I go back to my tree now."

Helene watched the Kamazili Pygmy disappear on the opposite side of the clearing. Then she turned and entered the plane to see how Berta was doing.

"Honestly," said the woman, after they had talked for a brief while, "I don't know what I was doing out there. I vaguely recall going out to find you and the Pygmy. I do not know why."

"Perhaps you were sleep walking," suggested Helene.

"Perhaps," nodded Berta.

"It is a couple of hours before dawn," said Helene. "Let's see if we can get some sleep and be ready to leave shortly after the sun comes up."

A few hours later, the Lockheed Vega was droning east.

Berta had positioned herself where she could watch Helene as she took off that morning and N'Geeso was situated where he could watch both women.

"Down there," exclaimed the jungle woman, "is the clearing where this all started!"

The area was visible for only a few moments and then they were beyond it. Helene adjusted her flight and was now turning more toward the north-east.

"Are you going to that Masai village you had talked about?" asked Berta.

"Yes," replied Helene. "Their chief is Tembu George. He is an American and he will help us. He will send for a plane to come out with petrol so that this plane can be flown on to Nairobi."

"Will you fly it?" asked Berta.

"No, I do not plan to," was the reply. "George will have another pilot brought out and they will fly both planes back. All you have to do is just ride along."

It was not long before Helene was throttling down in preparation for landing. There was a large open area where the Masai *kraal* was located and she picked a place that seemingly did not have anyone or anything in it. As she landed the Lockheed Vega, she realized Berta was practically leaning over her shoulder, watching everything she was doing.

As the three travelers stepped down from the plane, they saw a number of the tall Masai coming toward them. The man in the lead had a .45 automatic belted about his waist and a golden chain glittered about his neck.

"There is Tembu George!" exclaimed Helene and she shouted to the big chief trotting toward them.

Introductions were made and they started toward the village as Helene explained what the situation was with the plane and how she happened to be flying it.

They were near the *kraal* gate when Berta gave a gasp. "I forgot some-thing!" she exclaimed. "I've got to get it! I'll be right back!"

Without listening to anyone, she turned and ran back to the Lockheed Vega. The small crowd watched her go, most with dismay on their faces. Oh, well, white people were very unpredictable.

They were about to enter the *kraal* when they heard the engine of the Lockheed Vega roar into life. They all turned toward the craft. Helene Vaughn had a look of surprise on her face.

"I guess that woman could fly, after all," she said as the plane turned and taxied into the wind.

"That woman evil," said N'Geeso. "She big gangster!"

Then the plane left the ground but it did not level off. Instead it made a big loop and looked like it was going to crash nose first just a few hundred yards away. But it came out of the loop just before smashing and went into another loop, much larger than the first one.

The second loop went very high and beyond the village. When the airplane was coming down, nose first, it did not pull up. There was a loud splash and the sound of the motor sputtering before it died.

The Masai, along with Helene and N'Geeso, hurried the several hundred yards to the Maracuzo River. It was some distance from the village, so no one was in the area when it crashed, but when the group arrived, only the tail section was sticking out of the fast moving, swirling water.

"It is stuck nose first in the bottom of the river," exclaimed Tembu George. "I do not believe you need petrol or pilots now, Helene," the big chief said.

"We need to check and see if Berta is still alive!" exclaimed Helene.

"No," said Tembu George, "the current is strong and she has been under water for several minutes already. It would take good swimmers several more minutes to reach her. There is nothing any of us can do."

That afternoon, before leaving the Masai, Helene drew Tembu George to one side. "I want to tell you this," she said, "but I don't think you want to tell your people. On that plane were three burlap backpacks stuffed with treasure. Berta thought she had it hidden and that we did not know about it. That was the purpose of her trying to take off in the plane. There is a fortune there, but it would probably cost several lives to try and recover it."

"That is true," said the Masai chief. "It can just remain where it is."

"Thanks," smiled Helene.

That afternoon they walked to the Maracuza River to see the Silver Bird one last time before beginning their journey south and home.

To their surprise, it was gone.

"The current is strong," said Tembu George. "It is now at the bottom and the river could be moving it along down stream. Eventually it may be covered with mud. The hull will rot and the motor will rust. The Silver Bird is gone."

THE END

WHY THE JUNGLE LORD?

First and foremost, I have been a Tarzan collector for sixty plus years. Writing a Tarzan story for publication would, of course, be totally off-limits for someone like myself. When the opportunity came up to write a Ki-Gor story, I was very excited.

In my collection, I have a run of the *Jungle Stories* pulp magazine where Ki-Gor made an appearance in each issue. I believe I am missing four out of the fifty-nine issue run. Rereading some of those old stories was a pleasant experience. They were much better written than I had remembered them. I think my early memories were the result of Ki-Gor not actually being Tarzan. Therefore, they couldn't be as good. No, they're not as good as Burroughs' Tarzan. But they are still good stories.

I like to write. I like to tell stories. I have written a number of jungle stories and I thought, at first, that I would just convert one of them. But I didn't feel right doing that. In my case, it is just a matter of doing some more daydreaming. It is easy to dream up something but it is another matter to put it on paper and make it readable.

As I write, I generally have several different avenues the character can take to reach the conclusion. It has to feel right when I reach that junction of the story. It also has to fit the character of the character!

If I have done a good job in working out the story then it doesn't take me too long to get it on paper. If I get in a hurry and try to start writing before I have it figured out, then the writing becomes a struggle. But I don't usually struggle.

ABOUT OUR CREATORS

WRITER -

JOHN R. ROSE is a retired school teacher. He was born at the end of the Dust Bowl era and raised in south central Kansas. He came from a sandhill farm with seven siblings where there was always work to be done. They did not participate in 4-H, Boy Scouts, or Little League Baseball as that meant someone had to take off work to drive you there and be on hand to bring you home. Nope, the big entertainment was going to the library while the parents were in town buying groceries.

Some of the early work children could do included bugging potato plants, hoeing corn, carrying water to hogs, milking cows and feeding calves. This was all the kind of work where you could daydream about the characters you had been reading about. When the author started to high school he became involved in sports, including football, basketball and track. Later he attended and graduated from college using help from athletic scholarships to make it through financially. With that background, many of his stories will include segments where the characters are involved in athletics.

John is married and the father of a son and a daughter, both of whom are grown and gone from home. His wife often pulls him away from the keyboard to accompany her on trips around the country and abroad. He has been in every state in the Union, except one, but expects to get that one in the days ahead.

INTERIOR ILLUSTRATOR –

CLAYTON HINKLE is a life-long, self taught (for the most part) artist whose main ambition in life is to basically draw cool, adventurous, fantastic, horrorific Pulp and Comic art. Most, if not all, of his published work has been in the new Pulps of today, Air Ship 27 Productions being the major outlet of his wares by far, as well as work for the fanzine "REH, Two-Gun

Raconteur", a 'zine dedicated to the late, great Robert E. Howard and his works. He hopes to one day make his living by drawing, pure and simple.

COVER ARTIST –

ANDY FISH is a writer and artist of graphic novels and comic books. He has a lifelong passion for serials and pulp magazines which is why he is thrilled to be providing art and covers for Airship 27. His latest graphic novel, DRACULA'S ARMY from McFarland Press was released during the Halloween 2013 season. Andy is delighted to be working with the Airship 27 team. You can visit his website at-www.andytfish.com

Making Pulp History!

From the heart of Africa to the streets of Harlem, a new hero is born sworn to support and protect Americans of all races and creeds; he is Damballa and he strikes from the shadows. When the reigning black heavy weight boxing champion of the world agrees to defend his crown against a German fighter representing Hitler's Nazi regime, the ring becomes the stage for a greater political contest. The Nazis' agenda is to humble the American champion and prove the superiority of their pure-blood Aryan heritage. To achieve this end, they employ an unscrupulous scientist capable of transforming their warrior into a superhuman killing machine.

Can the mysterious Damballa unravel their insidious plot before it is too late to save a brave and noble man? Airship 27 Productions and Cornerstone Book Publishers are proud to introduce pulpdom's first ever 1930s African-American pulp hero as created by the acclaimed author, Charles Saunders.

"Having revolutionized the genre of epic fantasy with the creation of Imaro, a black warrior easily equal to such classic characters as Tarzan and Conan, Charles Saunders has done it again. This time he has created DAMBALLA, a true hero in every sense of the word. Battling racism and evil in the 1930's, DAMBALLA is no pale imitation of The Shadow or The Avenger. In fact, after reading this excellent book, I think that they would be proud to consider him a brother in the ceaseless war against crime and injustice." – Derrick Ferguson – "Dillon and the Voice of Odin"

Airship 27 Productions –

PULP FICTION FOR A NEW GENERATION!

AN AIRSHIP 27 PRODUCTION
CORNERSTONE BOOK PUBLISHERS
NEW PULP

Available at fine bookstores world-wide, at Gopulp.info, or as a PDF for your eReader at Airship27hangar.com

www.ingramcontent.com/pod-product-compliance
Lightning Source LLC
Chambersburg PA
CBHW071241250626
47163CB00001B/274